Adventures of a Gentleman Thief

Maurice Leblanc

Cherry Stone Publishing, an imprint of
Sweet Cherry Publishing Limited
Unit 36, Vulcan House,
Vulcan Road,
Leicester, LE5 3EF
United Kingdom

First published by Cherry Stone Publishing in 2021
2021 edition

2 4 6 8 10 9 7 5 3 1

ISBN: 978-1-78226-538-2

© Sweet Cherry Publishing

Adventures of a Gentleman Thief:
The Extraordinary Adventures of Arsène Lupin

Originally written in French by Maurice Leblanc.

Cover design by Jess Brown

www.cherrystonepublishing.com

Printed and bound in Turkey
T.IO006

The Extraordinary Adventures of Arsène Lupin

Maurice Leblanc

CHERRY STONE
PUBLISHING

THE ARREST OF ARSÈNE LUPIN

It was a strange ending to a voyage that had commenced in a most auspicious manner. The transatlantic steamship 'La Provence' was a swift and comfortable vessel, under the command of a most affable man. The passengers constituted a select and delightful society. The charm of new acquaintances and improvised amusements served to make the time pass agreeably. We enjoyed the pleasant sensation of being separated from the world, living, as it were, upon an unknown island, and consequently obliged to be sociable with each other.

Have you ever stopped to consider how much originality and spontaneity emanate from these various individuals who, on the preceding evening did not even know each other, and who are now, for several days, condemned to lead a life of extreme intimacy, jointly defying the anger of the ocean, the terrible onslaught of the waves, the violence of the tempest and the agonizing monotony of the calm and sleepy water? Such a life becomes a sort of tragic existence, with its storms and its grandeurs, its monotony and its diversity; and that is why, perhaps, we embark upon that short voyage with mingled feelings of pleasure and fear.

But, over the past few years, a new sensation has been added to the life of the transatlantic traveller. The little floating island is now attached to the world from which it was once quite free. A bond unites them, even in the very heart of the watery wastes of the Atlantic. That bond is the wireless telegraph, by means of which we receive news in the most mysterious manner. We know full well that the message is not transported by the medium of a hollow wire. No, the mystery is even more inexplicable, more romantic, and we must have recourse to the wings of the air in order to explain this new miracle. During the first day of the voyage, we felt that we were being followed, escorted, preceded even, by that distant voice, which, from time to time, whispered to one of us a few words from the receding world. Two friends spoke to me. Ten, twenty others sent gay or sombre words of parting to other passengers.

On the second day, at a distance of five hundred miles from the French coast, in the midst of a violent storm, we received the following message by means of the wireless telegraph:

Arsène Lupin is on your vessel, first cabin, blonde hair, wound right fore-arm, travelling alone under name of R ...

At that moment, a terrible flash of lightning rent the stormy skies. The electric waves were interrupted. The remainder of the dispatch never reached us. Of the name under which Arsène Lupin was concealing himself, we knew only the initial.

If the news had been of some other character, I have no doubt that the secret would have been carefully guarded by the telegraphic operator as well as by the officers of the vessel. But it was one of those events calculated to escape from the most rigorous discretion. The same day, no one knew how, the incident became a matter of current gossip and every passenger was aware that the famous Arsène Lupin was hiding in our midst.

Arsène Lupin in our midst! The irresponsible burglar whose exploits had been narrated in all the newspapers during the past few months! The mysterious individual with whom Ganimard, our shrewdest detective, had been engaged in an implacable conflict amidst interesting and picturesque surroundings. Arsène Lupin, the eccentric gentleman who operates only in the châteaux and salons and who, one night, entered the residence of Baron Schormann but emerged empty-handed, leaving, however, his card on which he had scribbled these words: 'Arsène Lupin, gentleman-burglar, will return when the furniture is genuine.' Arsène Lupin, the man of a thousand disguises: in turn a chauffeur, detective, bookmaker, Russian physician, Spanish bull-fighter, commercial traveller, robust youth, or decrepit old man.

Then consider this startling situation: Arsène Lupin was wandering about within the limited bounds of a transatlantic steamer; in that very small corner of the world, in that dining saloon, in that smoking room, in that music room! Arsène Lupin was, perhaps, this gentleman ... or that one ... my neighbour at the table ... the sharer of my stateroom ...

"And this condition of affairs will last for five days!" exclaimed Miss Nelly Underdown, the next morning. "It is unbearable! I hope he will be arrested."

Then, addressing me, she added:

"And you, Monsieur d'Andrézy, you are on intimate terms with the captain; surely you know something?"

I should have been delighted had I possessed any information that would interest Miss Nelly. She was one of those magnificent creatures who inevitably attract attention in every assembly. Wealth and beauty form an irresistible combination, and Nelly possessed both.

Educated in Paris under the care of a French mother, she was now going to visit her father, the millionaire Underdown of Chicago. She was accompanied by one of her friends, Lady Jerland.

At first, I had decided to open a flirtation with her; but, in the rapidly growing intimacy of the voyage, I was soon impressed by her charming manner and my feelings became too deep and reverential for a mere flirtation. Moreover, she accepted my attentions with a certain degree of favour. She condescended to laugh at my witticisms and display an interest in my stories. Yet I felt that I had a rival in the person of a young man with quiet and refined tastes; and it struck me, at times, that she preferred his taciturn humour to my Parisian frivolity. He formed one in the circle of admirers that surrounded Miss Nelly at the time she addressed to me the foregoing question. We were all comfortably seated in our deck-chairs. The storm of the preceding evening had cleared the sky.

The weather was now delightful.

"I have no definite knowledge, mademoiselle," I replied, "but cannot we, ourselves, investigate the mystery quite as well as the detective Ganimard, the personal enemy of Arsène Lupin?"

"Oh! oh! you are progressing very fast, monsieur."

"Not at all, mademoiselle. In the first place, let me ask, do you find the problem a complicated one?"

"Very complicated."

"Have you forgotten the key we hold for the solution to the problem?"

"What key?"

"In the first place, Lupin calls himself Monsieur R–"

"Rather vague information," she replied.

"Secondly, he is travelling alone."

"Does that help you?" she asked.

"Thirdly, he is blonde."

"Well?"

"Then we have only to peruse the passenger list, and proceed by process of elimination."

I had that list in my pocket. I took it out and glanced through it. Then I remarked:

"I find that there are only thirteen men on the passenger-list whose names begin with the letter R."

"Only thirteen?"

"Yes, in the first cabin. And of those thirteen, I find that nine of them are accompanied by women, children or servants. That leaves only four who are travelling alone. First, the Marquis de Raverdan–"

"Secretary to the American Ambassador," interrupted Miss Nelly. "I know him."

"Major Rawson," I continued.

"He is my uncle," someone said.

"Monsieur Rivolta."

"Here!" exclaimed an Italian, whose face was concealed beneath a heavy black beard.

Miss Nelly burst into laughter, and exclaimed: "That gentleman can scarcely be called a blonde."

"Very well, then," I said, "we are forced to the conclusion that the guilty party is the last one on the list."

"What is his name?"

"Monsieur Rozaine. Does anyone know him?"

No one answered. But Miss Nelly turned to the taciturn young man, whose attentions to her had annoyed me, and said:

"Well, Monsieur Rozaine, why do you not answer?"

All eyes were now turned upon him. He was a blond. I must confess that I myself felt a shock of surprise, and the profound silence that followed her question indicated that the others present also viewed the situation with a feeling of sudden alarm. However, the idea was an absurd one, because the gentleman in question presented an air of the most perfect innocence.

"Why do I not answer?" he said. "Because, considering my name, my position as a solitary traveller and the colour of my hair, I have already reached the same conclusion, and now think that I should be arrested."

He presented a strange appearance as he uttered these words. His thin lips were drawn closer than usual and his face was ghastly pale, whilst his eyes were streaked with blood. Of course, he was joking, yet his appearance and attitude impressed us strangely.

"But you have not the wound?" said Miss Nelly, naively.

"That is true," he replied, "I lack the wound."

Then he pulled up his sleeve, removing his cuff, and showed us his arm. But that action did not deceive me. He had shown us his left arm, and I was on the point of calling his attention to the fact, when another incident diverted our attention. Lady Jerland, Miss Nelly's friend, came running towards us in a state of great excitement, exclaiming:

"My jewels, my pearls! Someone has stolen them all!"

No, they were not all gone, as we soon found out. The thief had taken only part of them; a very curious thing. Of the diamond sunbursts, jewelled pendants, bracelets and necklaces, the thief had taken, not the largest but the finest and most valuable stones. The mountings were lying upon the table. I saw them there, despoiled of their jewels, like flowers from which the beautiful coloured petals had been ruthlessly plucked. And this theft must have been committed at the time Lady Jerland was taking her tea; in broad daylight, in a stateroom opening on a much-frequented corridor; moreover, the thief had been obliged to force open the door of the stateroom, search for the jewel case, which was hidden at the bottom of a hat box, open it, select his booty and remove it from the mountings.

Of course, all the passengers instantly reached the same conclusion; it was the work of Arsène Lupin.

That day, at the dinner table, the seats to the right and left of Rozaine remained vacant; and, during the evening, it was rumoured that the captain had placed him under arrest, which information produced a feeling of safety and relief. We breathed once more. That evening, we resumed our games and dances. Miss Nelly, especially, displayed a spirit of thoughtless gaiety which convinced me that if Rozaine's attentions had been agreeable to her in the beginning, she had already forgotten them. Her charm and good-humour completed my conquest. At midnight, under a bright moon, I declared my devotion with an ardour that did not seem to displease her.

But, the next day, to our general amazement, Rozaine was at liberty. We learned that the evidence against him was not sufficient. He had produced documents that were perfectly regular, which showed that he was the son of a wealthy merchant of Bordeaux. Besides, his arms did not bear the slightest trace of a wound.

"Documents! Certificates of birth!" exclaimed the enemies of Rozaine, "of course, Arsène Lupin will furnish you as many as you desire. And as to the wound, he never had it, or he has removed it."

Then it was proven that, at the time of the theft, Rozaine was promenading on the deck. To which fact, his enemies replied that a man like Arsène Lupin could commit a crime without being actually present. And then, apart from all other circumstances, there remained one point which even the most sceptical could not answer: who except Rozaine, was travelling alone, was a blond, and bore a name beginning with R? To whom did the telegram point, if it were not Rozaine?

And when Rozaine, a few minutes before breakfast, came boldly toward our group, Miss Nelly and Lady Jerland arose and walked away.

An hour later, a manuscript circular was passed from hand to hand amongst the sailors, the stewards, and the passengers of all classes. It announced that Monsieur Louis Rozaine offered a reward of ten thousand francs for the discovery of Arsène Lupin or other person in possession of the stolen jewels.

"And if no one assists me, I will unmask the scoundrel myself," declared Rozaine.

Rozaine against Arsène Lupin, or rather, according to current opinion, Arsène Lupin himself against Arsène Lupin; the contest promised to be interesting.

Nothing developed during the next two days. We saw Rozaine wandering about, day and night, searching, questioning, investigating. The captain, also, displayed commendable activity. He caused the vessel to be searched from stem to stern; ransacked every stateroom under the plausible theory that the jewels might be concealed anywhere, except in the thief's own room.

"I suppose they will find out something soon," remarked Miss Nelly to me. "He may be a wizard, but he cannot make diamonds and pearls become invisible."

"Certainly not," I replied, "but he should examine the lining of our hats and vests and everything we carry with us."

Then, exhibiting my Kodak, a 9x12 with which I had been photographing her in various poses, I added: "In an apparatus no larger than this, a person could hide all of Lady Jerland's jewels. He could pretend to take pictures and no one would suspect the game."

"But I have heard it said that every thief leaves some clue behind him."

"That may be generally true," I replied, "but there is one exception: Arsène Lupin."

"Why?"

"Because he concentrates his thoughts not only on the theft, but on all the circumstances connected with it that could serve as a clue to his identity."

"A few days ago, you were more confident."

"Yes, but since then I have seen him at work."

"And what do you think about it now?" she asked.

"Well, in my opinion, we are wasting our time."

And, as a matter of fact, the investigation had produced no result. But, in the meantime, the captain's watch had been stolen. He was furious. He quickened his efforts and watched Rozaine more closely than before. But, on the following day, the watch was found in the second officer's collar box.

This incident caused considerable astonishment, and displayed the humorous side of Arsène Lupin, burglar though he was, but dilettante as well. He combined business with pleasure. He reminded us of the author who almost died in a fit of laughter provoked by his own play. Certainly, he was an artist in his particular line of work, and whenever I saw Rozaine, gloomy and reserved, and thought of the double role that he was playing, I accorded him a certain measure of admiration.

On the following evening, the officer on deck duty heard groans emanating from the darkest corner of the ship. He approached and found a man lying there, his head enveloped in a thick grey scarf and his hands tied together with a heavy cord. It was Rozaine. He had been assaulted, thrown down and robbed. A card, pinned to his coat, bore these words: 'Arsène Lupin accepts with pleasure the ten thousand francs offered by Monsieur Rozaine.' As a matter of fact, the stolen pocket-book contained twenty thousand francs.

Of course, some accused the unfortunate man of having simulated this attack on himself. But, apart from the fact that he could not have bound himself in that manner, it was established that the writing on the card was entirely different from that of Rozaine, but, on the contrary, resembled the handwriting of Arsène Lupin as it was reproduced in an old newspaper found on board.

Thus it appeared that Rozaine was not Arsène Lupin; but was Rozaine, the son of a Bordeaux merchant. And the presence of Arsène Lupin was once more affirmed, and that in a most alarming manner.

Such was the state of terror amongst the passengers that none would remain alone in a stateroom or wander singly in unfrequented parts of the vessel. We clung together as a matter of safety. And yet the most intimate acquaintances were estranged by a mutual feeling of distrust. Arsène Lupin was, now, anybody and everybody. Our excited imaginations attributed to him miraculous and unlimited power. We supposed him capable of assuming the most unexpected disguises; of being, by turns, the highly respectable Major Rawson or the noble Marquis de Raverdan, or even – for we no longer stopped with the accusing letter of R – or even such or such a person well known to all of us, and having wife, children and servants.

The first wireless dispatches from America brought no news; at least, the captain did not communicate any to us.

The silence was not reassuring.

Our last day on the steamer seemed interminable. We lived in constant fear of some disaster. This time, it would not be a simple theft or a comparatively harmless assault; it would be a crime, a murder. No one imagined that Arsène Lupin would confine himself to those two trifling offenses. Absolute master of the ship, the authorities powerless, he could do whatever he pleased; our property and lives were at his mercy.

Yet those were delightful hours for me, since they secured to me the confidence of Miss Nelly. Deeply moved by those startling events and being of a highly nervous nature, she spontaneously sought at my side a protection and security that I was pleased to give her. Inwardly, I blessed Arsène Lupin. Had he not been the means of bringing me and Miss Nelly closer to each other? Thanks to him, I could now indulge in delicious dreams of love and happiness – dreams that, I felt, were not unwelcome to Miss Nelly. Her smiling eyes authorized me to make them; the softness of her voice bade me hope.

As we approached the American shore, the active search for the thief was apparently abandoned, and we were anxiously awaiting the supreme moment in which the mysterious enigma would be explained. Who was Arsène Lupin? Under what name, under what disguise was the famous Arsène Lupin concealing himself? And, at last, that supreme moment arrived. If I live one hundred years, I shall not forget the slightest details of it.

"How pale you are, Miss Nelly," I said to my companion, as she leaned upon my arm, almost fainting.

"And you!" she replied, "Ah! You are so changed."

"Just think! This is a most exciting moment, and I am delighted to spend it with you, Miss Nelly. I hope that your memory will sometimes revert–"

But she was not listening. She was nervous and excited. The gangway was placed in position, but, before we could use it, the uniformed customs officers came on board. Miss Nelly murmured:

"I shouldn't be surprised to hear that Arsène Lupin escaped from the vessel during the voyage."

"Perhaps he preferred death to dishonour, and plunged into the Atlantic rather than be arrested."

"Oh, do not laugh," she said.

Suddenly I started, and, in answer to her question, I said:

"Do you see that little old man standing at the bottom of the gangway?"

"With an umbrella and an olive-green coat?"

"It is Ganimard."

"Ganimard?"

"Yes, the celebrated detective who has sworn to capture Arsène Lupin. Ah! I can understand now why we did not receive any news from this side of the Atlantic. Ganimard was here! And he always keeps his business secret."

"Then you think he will arrest Arsène Lupin?"

"Who can tell? The unexpected always happens when Arsène Lupin is concerned in the affair."

"Oh!" she exclaimed, with that morbid curiosity peculiar to women, "I should like to see him arrested."

"You will have to be patient. No doubt, Arsène Lupin

has already seen his enemy and will not be in a hurry to leave the steamer."

The passengers were now leaving the steamer. Leaning on his umbrella, with an air of careless indifference, Ganimard appeared to be paying no attention to the crowd that was hurrying down the gangway. The Marquis de Raverdan, Major Rawson, the Italian Rivolta, and many others had already left the vessel before Rozaine appeared. Poor Rozaine!

"Perhaps it is he, after all," said Miss Nelly to me. "What do you think?"

"I think it would be very interesting to have Ganimard and Rozaine in the same picture. You take the camera. I am loaded down."

I gave her the camera, but too late for her to use it. Rozaine was already passing the detective. An American officer, standing behind Ganimard, leaned forwards and whispered in his ear. The French detective shrugged his shoulders and Rozaine passed on. Then, my God, who was Arsène Lupin?

"Yes," said Miss Nelly, aloud, "who can it be?"

Not more than twenty people now remained on board. She scrutinized them one by one, fearful that Arsène Lupin was not amongst them.

"We cannot wait much longer," I said to her.

She started toward the gangway. I followed. But we had not taken ten steps when Ganimard barred our passage.

"Well, what is it?" I exclaimed.

"One moment, monsieur. What's your hurry?"

"I am escorting mademoiselle."

"One moment," he repeated, in a tone of authority. Then, gazing into my eyes, he said:

"Arsène Lupin, is it not?"

I laughed, and replied: "No, simply Bernard d'Andrézy."

"Bernard d'Andrézy died in Macedonia three years ago."

"If Bernard d'Andrézy were dead, I should not be here. But you are mistaken. Here are my papers."

"They are his; and I can tell you exactly how they came into your possession."

"You are a fool!" I exclaimed. "Arsène Lupin sailed under the name of R–"

"Yes, another of your tricks; a false scent that deceived them at Havre. You play a good game, my boy, but this time luck is against you."

I hesitated a moment. Then he hit me a sharp blow on the right arm, which caused me to utter a cry of pain. He had struck the wound, yet unhealed, referred to in the telegram.

I was obliged to surrender. There was no alternative. I turned to Miss Nelly, who had heard everything. Our eyes met; then she glanced at the Kodak I had placed in her hands, and made a gesture that conveyed to me the impression that she understood everything. Yes, there, between the narrow folds of black leather, in the hollow centre of the small object that I had taken the precaution to place in her hands before Ganimard arrested me, it was there I had deposited Rozaine's twenty thousand francs and Lady Jerland's pearls and diamonds.

Oh! I pledge my oath that, at that solemn moment, when I was in the grasp of Ganimard and his two assistants, I was perfectly indifferent to everything, to my arrest, the hostility of the people, everything except this one question: what will Miss Nelly do with the things I had confided to her?

In the absence of that material and conclusive proof, I had nothing to fear; but would Miss Nelly decide to furnish that proof? Would she betray me? Would she act the part of an enemy who cannot forgive, or that of a woman whose scorn is softened by feelings of indulgence and involuntary sympathy?

She passed in front of me. I said nothing, but bowed very low. Mingled with the other passengers, she advanced to the gangway with my Kodak in her hand. It occurred to me that she would not dare to expose me publicly, but she might do so when she reached a more private place. However, when she had passed only a few feet down the gangway, with a movement of simulated awkwardness, she let the camera fall into the water between the vessel and the pier. Then she walked down the gangway, and was quickly lost to sight in the crowd. She had passed out of my life forever.

For a moment, I stood motionless. Then, to Ganimard's great astonishment, I muttered:

"What a pity that I am not an honest man!"

* * *

Such was the story of his arrest as narrated to me by Arsène Lupin himself. The various incidents, which I shall record in writing at a later day, have established between us certain ties ... shall I say of friendship? Yes, I venture to believe that Arsène Lupin honours me with his friendship, and that it is through friendship that he occasionally calls on me, and brings, into the silence of my library, his youthful exuberance of spirits, the contagion of his enthusiasm, and the mirth of a man for whom destiny has naught but favours and smiles.

His portrait? How can I describe him? I have seen him twenty times and each time he was a different person; even he himself said to me on one occasion: "I no longer know who I am. I cannot recognize myself in the mirror." Certainly, he was a great actor, and possessed a marvellous faculty for disguising himself. Without the slightest effort, he could adopt the voice, gestures and mannerisms of another person.

"Why," said he, "why should I retain a definite form and feature? Why not avoid the danger of a personality that is ever the same? My actions will serve to identify me."

Then he added, with a touch of pride:

"So much the better if no one can ever say with absolute certainty: There is Arsène Lupin! The essential point is that the public may be able to refer to my work and say, without fear of mistake: Arsène Lupin did that!"

Arsène Lupin
in Prison

There is no tourist worthy of the name who does not know the banks of the Seine, and has not noticed, in passing, the little feudal castle of the Malaquis, built upon a rock in the centre of the river. An arched bridge connects it with the shore. All around it, the calm waters of the great river play peacefully amongst the reeds, and the wagtails flutter over the moist crests of the stones.

The history of the Malaquis castle is stormy like its name, harsh like its outlines. It has passed through a long series of combats, sieges, assaults, rapines and massacres. A recital of the crimes that have been committed there would cause the stoutest heart to tremble. There are many mysterious legends connected with the castle, and they tell us of a famous subterranean tunnel that formerly led to the abbey of Jumieges and to the manor of Agnes Sorel, mistress of Charles VII.

In that ancient habitation of heroes and brigands, the Baron Nathan Cahorn now lived; or Baron Satan as he was formerly called on the Bourse, where he had acquired a fortune with incredible rapidity. The lords of Malaquis, absolutely ruined, had been obliged to sell the ancient castle at a great sacrifice. It contained an admirable collection of furniture, pictures, wood carvings, and faience. The Baron lived there alone, attended by three old servants. No one ever entered the place. No one had ever beheld the three Rubens that he possessed, his two Watteau, his Jean Goujon pulpit, and the many other treasures that he had acquired by a vast expenditure of money at public sales.

Baron Satan lived in constant fear, not for himself, but for the treasures that he had accumulated with such an earnest devotion and with so much perspicacity that the shrewdest merchant could not say that the Baron had ever erred in his taste or judgment. He loved them – his bibelots. He loved them intensely, like a miser; jealously, like a lover. Every day, at sunset, the iron gates at either end of the bridge and at the entrance to the court of honour are closed and barred. At the least touch on these gates, electric bells will ring throughout the castle.

One Thursday in September, a postal worker presented himself at the gate at the head of the bridge, and, as usual, it was the Baron himself who partially opened the heavy portal. He scrutinized the man as minutely as if he were a stranger, although the honest face and twinkling eyes of the postman had been familiar to the Baron for many years. The man laughed, as he said:

"It is only I, Monsieur le Baron. It is not another man wearing my cap and blouse."

"One can never tell," muttered the Baron.

The man handed him a number of newspapers, and then said:

"And now, Monsieur le Baron, here is something new."

"Something new?"

"Yes, a letter. A registered letter."

Living as a recluse, without friends or business relations, the baron never received any letters, and the one now presented to him immediately aroused within him a feeling of suspicion and distrust. It was like an evil omen. Who was this mysterious correspondent that dared to disturb the tranquillity of his retreat?

"You must sign for it, Monsieur le Baron."

He signed; then took the letter, waited until the postman had disappeared beyond the bend in the road, and, after walking nervously to and fro for a few minutes, he leaned against the parapet of the bridge and opened the envelope. It contained a sheet of paper, bearing this heading: Prison de la Santé, Paris. He looked at the signature: Arsène Lupin. Then he read:

Monsieur le Baron:

There is, in the gallery in your castle, a picture of Philippe de Champaigne, of exquisite finish, which pleases me beyond measure. Your Rubens are also to my taste, as well as your smallest Watteau. In the salon to the right, I have noticed the Louis XIII cadence-table, the tapestries of Beauvais, the Empire gueridon signed 'Jacob,' and the Renaissance chest. In the salon to the left, all the cabinet full of jewels and miniatures.

For the present, I will content myself with those articles that can be conveniently removed. I will therefore ask you to pack them carefully and ship them to me, charges prepaid, to the station at Batignolles,

*within eight days, otherwise I shall be obliged to remove
them myself during the night of 27 September; but,
under those circumstances, I shall not content myself
with the articles above mentioned.*

*Accept my apologies for any inconvenience I may
cause you, and believe me to be your humble servant,*
Arsène Lupin.

*P. S. —Please do not send the largest Watteau.
Although you paid thirty thousand francs for it, it is
only a copy, the original having been burned under
the Directoire by Barras, during a night of debauchery.
Consult the memoirs of Garat.*

*I do not care for the Louis XV chatelaine, as I doubt
its authenticity.*

That letter completely upset the baron. Had it borne
any other signature, he would have been greatly alarmed –
but signed by Arsène Lupin!

As a habitual reader of the newspapers, he was versed
in the history of recent crimes, and was therefore well
acquainted with the exploits of the mysterious burglar.
Of course, he knew that Lupin had been arrested in
America by his enemy Ganimard and was at present
incarcerated in the Prison de la Santé. But he knew
also that any miracle might be expected from Arsène
Lupin. Moreover, that exact knowledge of the castle,
the location of the pictures and furniture, gave the
affair an alarming aspect. How could he have acquired
that information concerning things that no one had
ever seen?

The baron raised his eyes and contemplated the stern

outlines of the castle, its steep rocky pedestal, the depth of the surrounding water, and shrugged his shoulders. Certainly, there was no danger. No one in the world could force an entrance to the sanctuary that contained his priceless treasures.

No one, perhaps, but Arsène Lupin! For him, gates, walls and drawbridges did not exist. What use were the most formidable obstacles or the most careful precautions, if Arsène Lupin had decided to affect an entrance?

That evening, he wrote to the Procurer of the Republique at Rouen. He enclosed the threatening letter and solicited aid and protection.

The reply came at once to the effect that Arsène Lupin was in custody in the Prison de la Santé, under close surveillance, with no opportunity to write such a letter, which was, no doubt, the work of some imposter. But, as an act of precaution, the Procurer had submitted the letter to an expert in handwriting, who declared that in spite of certain resemblances, the writing was not that of the prisoner.

But the words 'in spite of certain resemblances' caught the attention of the baron; in them, he read the possibility of a doubt which appeared to him quite sufficient to warrant the intervention of the law. His fears increased. He read Lupin's letter over and over again. 'I shall be obliged to remove them myself.' And then there was the fixed date: the night of 27 September.

To confide in his servants was a proceeding repugnant to his nature; but now, for the first time in many years, he experienced the necessity of seeking counsel with someone. Abandoned by the legal official of his own district, and feeling unable to defend himself with his own resources, he was on the point of going to Paris to engage the services of a detective.

Two days passed; on the third day, he was filled with hope and joy as he read the following item in the *Réveil de Caudebec*, a newspaper published in a neighbouring town:

> *We have the pleasure of entertaining in our city, at the present time, the veteran detective Monsieur Ganimard who acquired a world-wide reputation by his clever capture of Arsène Lupin. He has come here for rest and recreation, and, being an enthusiastic fisherman, he threatens to capture all the fish in our river.*

Ganimard! Ah, here is the assistance desired by Baron Cahorn! Who could baffle the schemes of Arsène Lupin better than Ganimard, the patient and astute detective? He was the man for the place.

The baron did not hesitate. The town of Caudebec was only six kilometres from the castle, a short distance for a man whose step was accelerated by the hope of safety.

After several fruitless attempts to ascertain the detective's address, the baron visited the office of the *Réveil*, situated on the quay. There he found the writer of the article who, approaching the window, exclaimed:

"Ganimard? Why, you are sure to see him somewhere on the quay with his fishing-pole. I met him there and chanced to read his name engraved on his rod. Ah, there he is now, under the trees."

"That little man, wearing a straw hat?"

"Exactly. He is a gruff fellow, with little to say."

Five minutes later, the baron approached the celebrated Ganimard, introduced himself, and sought to commence a conversation, but that was a failure. Then he broached the real object of his interview, and briefly stated his case. The other listened, motionless, with his attention riveted on his fishing-rod. When the baron had finished his story, the fisherman turned, with an air of profound pity, and said:

"Monsieur, it is not customary for thieves to warn people they are about to rob. Arsène Lupin, especially, would not commit such a folly."

"But–"

"Monsieur, if I had the least doubt, believe me, the pleasure of again capturing Arsène Lupin would place me at your disposal. But, unfortunately, that young man is already under lock and key."

"He may have escaped."

"No one has ever escaped from the Santé."

"But, he–"

"He, no more than any other."

"Yet–"

"Well, if he escapes, so much the better. I will catch him again. Meanwhile, you go home and sleep soundly. That will do for the present. You frighten the fish."

The conversation was ended. The baron returned to the castle, reassured to some extent by Ganimard's indifference. He examined the bolts, watched the servants, and, during the next forty-eight hours, he became almost persuaded that his fears were groundless.

Certainly, as Ganimard had said, thieves do not warn people they are about to rob.

The fateful day was close at hand. It was now the twenty-sixth of September and nothing had happened. But at three o'clock the bell rang. A boy brought this telegram:

No goods at Batignolles station. Prepare everything for tomorrow night. Arsène.

This telegram threw the baron into such a state of excitement that he even considered the advisability of yielding to Lupin's demands.

However, he hastened to Caudebec. Ganimard was fishing at the same place, seated on a campstool. Without a word, he handed him the telegram.

"Well, what of it?" said the detective.

"What of it? But it is tomorrow."

"What is tomorrow?"

"The robbery! The pillage of my collections!"

Ganimard laid down his fishing-rod, turned to the baron, and exclaimed, in a tone of impatience:

"Ah! Do you think I am going to bother myself about such a silly story as that!"

"How much do you ask to pass tomorrow night in the castle?"

"Not a sou. Now, leave me alone."

"Name your own price. I am rich and can pay it."

This offer disconcerted Ganimard, who replied, calmly:

"I am here on a holiday. I have no right to undertake such work."

"No one will know. I promise to keep it secret."

"Oh! nothing will happen."

"Come! three thousand francs. Will that be enough?"

The detective, after a moment's reflection, said:

"Very well. But I must warn you that you are throwing your money out of the window."

"I do not care."

"In that case ... but, after all, what do we know about this devil Lupin! He may have quite a numerous band of robbers with him. Are you sure of your servants?"

"My faith—"

"Better not count on them. I will telegraph for two of my men to help me. And now, go! It is better for us not to be seen together. Tomorrow evening about nine o'clock."

* * *

The following day – the date fixed by Arsène Lupin – Baron Cahorn arranged all his panoply of war, furbished his weapons, and, like a sentinel, paced to and fro in front of the castle. He saw nothing, heard nothing. At half-past eight o'clock in the evening, he dismissed his servants. They occupied rooms in a wing of the building, in a retired spot, well removed from the main portion of the castle. Shortly thereafter, the baron heard the sound of approaching footsteps. It was Ganimard and his two assistants – great, powerful fellows with immense hands, and necks like bulls. After asking a few questions relating to the location of the various entrances and rooms, Ganimard carefully closed and barricaded all the doors and windows through which one could gain access to the threatened rooms. He inspected the walls, raised the tapestries, and finally installed his assistants in the central gallery which was located between the two salons.

"No nonsense! We are not here to sleep. At the slightest sound, open the windows of the court and call me. Pay attention also to the waterside. Ten metres of perpendicular rock is no obstacle to those devils."

Ganimard locked his assistants in the gallery, carried away the keys, and said to the baron:

"And now, to our post."

He had chosen for himself a small room located in the thick outer wall, between the two principal doors, and which, in former years, had been the watchman's quarters. A peephole opened upon the bridge; another on the court. In one corner, there was an opening to a tunnel.

"I believe you told me, Monsieur le Baron, that this tunnel is the only subterranean entrance to the castle and that it has been closed up for time immemorial?"

"Yes."

"Then, unless there is some other entrance, known only to Arsène Lupin, we are quite safe."

He placed three chairs together, stretched himself upon them, lighted his pipe and sighed:

"Really, Monsieur le Baron, I feel ashamed to accept your money for such a sinecure as this. I will tell the story to my friend Lupin. He will enjoy it immensely."

The baron did not laugh. He was anxiously listening, but heard nothing save the beating of his own heart. From time to time, he leaned over the tunnel and cast a fearful eye into its depths. He heard the clock strike eleven, twelve, one.

Suddenly, he seized Ganimard's arm. The latter leaped up, awakened from his sleep.

"Do you hear?" asked the baron, in a whisper.

"Yes."

"What is it?"

"I was snoring, I suppose."

"No, no, listen."

"Ah! Yes, it is the horn of an automobile."

"Well?"

"Well! it is very improbable that Lupin would use an automobile like a battering ram to demolish your castle. Come, Monsieur le Baron, return to your post. I am going to sleep. Goodnight."

That was the only alarm. Ganimard resumed his interrupted slumbers, and the baron heard nothing except the regular snoring of his companion. At break of day, they left the room. The castle was enveloped in a profound calm; it was a peaceful dawn on the bosom of a tranquil river. They mounted the stairs, Cahorn radiant with joy, Ganimard calm as usual. They heard no sound; they saw nothing to arouse suspicion.

"What did I tell you, Monsieur le Baron? Really, I should not have accepted your offer. I am ashamed."

He unlocked the door and entered the gallery. Upon two chairs, with drooping heads and pendent arms, the detective's two assistants were asleep.

"Tonnerre de nom d'un chien!" exclaimed Ganimard. At the same moment, the baron cried out:

"The pictures! The credence!"

He stammered, choked, with arms outstretched toward the empty places, toward the denuded walls where naught remained but the useless nails and cords. The Watteau, disappeared! The Rubens, carried away! The tapestries taken down! The cabinets, despoiled of their jewels!

"And my Louis XVI candelabra! And the Regent chandelier...! And my twelfth-century Virgin!"

He ran from one spot to another in wildest despair. He recalled the purchase price of each article, added up the figures, counted his losses, pell-mell, in confused words and unfinished phrases. He stamped with rage; he groaned with grief. He acted like a ruined man whose only hope is suicide.

If anything could have consoled him, it would have been the stupefaction displayed by Ganimard. The famous detective did not move. He appeared to be petrified; he examined the room in a listless manner. The windows ... closed. The locks on the doors ... intact. Not a break in the ceiling; not a hole in the floor. Everything was in perfect order. The theft had been carried out methodically, according to a logical and inexorable plan.

"Arsène Lupin ... Arsène Lupin," he muttered.

Suddenly, as if moved by anger, he rushed upon his two assistants and shook them violently. They did not awaken.

"The devil!" he cried. "Can it be possible?"

He leaned over them and, in turn, examined them closely. They were asleep; but their response was unnatural.

"They have been drugged," he said to the baron.

"By whom?"

"By him, of course, or his men under his discretion. That work bears his stamp."

"In that case, I am lost – nothing can be done."

"Nothing," assented Ganimard.

"It is dreadful; it is monstrous."

"Lodge a complaint."

"What good will that do?"

"Oh; it is well to try it. The law has some resources."

"The law! Bah! it is useless. You represent the law, and, at this moment, when you should be looking for a clue and trying to discover something, you do not even stir."

"Discover something with Arsène Lupin! Why, my dear monsieur, Arsène Lupin never leaves any clue behind him. He leaves nothing to chance. Sometimes I think he put himself in my way and simply allowed me to arrest him in America."

"Then, I must renounce my pictures! He has taken the gems of my collection. I would give a fortune to recover them. If there is no other way, let him name his own price."

Ganimard regarded the baron attentively, as he said:

"Now, that is sensible. Will you stick to it?"

"Yes, yes. But why?"

"An idea that I have."

"What is it?"

"We will discuss it later – if the official examination does not succeed. But, not one word about me, if you wish my assistance."

He added, between his teeth:

"It is true I have nothing to boast of in this affair."

The assistants were gradually regaining consciousness with the bewildered air of people who come out of an hypnotic sleep. They opened their eyes and looked about them in astonishment. Ganimard questioned them; they remembered nothing.

"But you must have seen someone?"

"No."

"Can't you remember?"

"No, no."

"Did you drink anything?"

They considered a moment, and then one of them replied:

"Yes, I drank a little water."

"Out of that carafe?"

"Yes."

"So did I," declared the other.

Ganimard smelled and tasted it. It had no particular taste and no odour.

"Come," he said, "we are wasting our time here. One can't decide an Arsène Lupin problem in five minutes. But, morbleu! I swear I will catch him again."

The same day, a charge of burglary was duly performed by Baron Cahorn against Arsène Lupin, a prisoner in the Prison de la Santé.

* * *

The baron afterwards regretted making the charge against Lupin when he saw his castle delivered over to the gendarmes, the procureur, the judge d'instruction, the newspaper reporters and photographers, and a throng of idle curiosity-seekers.

The affair soon became a topic of general discussion, and the name of Arsène Lupin excited the public imagination to such an extent that the newspapers filled their columns with the most fantastic stories of his exploits which found ready credence amongst their readers.

But the letter of Arsène Lupin that was published in the *Echo de France* (no one ever knew how the newspaper obtained it), that letter in which Baron Cahorn was impudently warned of the coming theft, caused considerable excitement. The most fabulous theories were advanced. Some recalled the existence of the famous subterranean tunnels, and that was the line of research pursued by the officers of the law, who searched the house from top to bottom, questioned every stone, studied the wainscoting and the chimneys, the window-frames and the girders in the ceilings. By the light of torches, they examined the immense cellars where the lords of Malaquis were wont to store their munitions and provisions. They sounded the rocky foundation to its very centre. But it was all in vain. They discovered no trace of a subterranean tunnel. No secret passage existed.

But the eager public declared that the pictures and furniture could not vanish like so many ghosts. They are substantial, material things and require doors and windows for their exits and their entrances, and so do the people that remove them. Who were those people? How did they gain access to the castle? And how did they leave it?

The police officers of Rouen, convinced of their own impotence, solicited the assistance of the Parisian detective force. Monsieur Dudouis, chief of the Sûreté, sent the best sleuths of the iron brigade. He himself spent forty-eight hours at the castle, but met with no success. Then he sent for Ganimard, whose past services had proved so useful when all else failed.

Ganimard listened, in silence, to the instructions of his superior; then, shaking his head, he said:

"In my opinion, it is useless to ransack the castle. The solution of the problem lies elsewhere."

"Where, then?"

"With Arsène Lupin."

"With Arsène Lupin! To support that theory, we must admit his intervention."

"I do admit it. In fact, I consider it quite certain."

"Come, Ganimard, that is absurd. Arsène Lupin is in prison."

"I grant you that Arsène Lupin is in prison, closely guarded; but he must have fetters on his feet, manacles on his wrists, and gag in his mouth before I change my opinion."

"Why so obstinate, Ganimard?"

"Because Arsène Lupin is the only man in France of sufficient calibre to invent and carry out a scheme of that magnitude."

"Mere words, Ganimard."

"But true ones. Look! What are they doing? Searching for subterranean passages, stones swinging on pivots, and other nonsense of that kind. But Lupin doesn't employ such old-fashioned methods. He is a modern cracksman, right up to date."

"And how would you proceed?"

"I should ask your permission to spend an hour with him."

"In his cell?"

"Yes. During the return trip from America we became very friendly, and I venture to say that if he can give me any information without compromising himself he will not hesitate to save me from incurring useless trouble."

It was shortly after noon when Ganimard entered the cell of Arsène Lupin. The latter, who was lying on his bed, raised his head and uttered a cry of apparent joy.

"Ah! This is a real surprise. My dear Ganimard, here!"

"Ganimard himself."

"In my chosen retreat, I have felt a desire for many things, but my fondest wish was to receive you here."

"Very kind of you, I am sure."

"Not at all. You know I hold you in the highest regard."

"I am proud of it."

"I have always said: Ganimard is our best detective. He is almost – you see how candid I am – he is almost as clever as Herlock Sholmes. But I am sorry that I cannot offer you anything better than this hard stool. And no refreshments! Not even a glass of beer! Of course, you will excuse me, as I am here only temporarily."

Ganimard smiled, and accepted the proffered seat. Then the prisoner continued:

"Mon Dieu, how pleased I am to see the face of an honest man. I am so tired of those devils of spies who come here ten times a day to ransack my pockets and my cell to satisfy themselves that I am not preparing to escape. The government is very solicitous on my account."

"It is quite right."

"Why so? I should be quite contented if they would allow me to live in my own quiet way."

"On other people's money."

"Quite so. That would be so simple. But here, I am joking, and you are, no doubt, in a hurry. So let us come to business, Ganimard. To what do I owe the honour of this visit?

"The Cahorn affair," declared Ganimard, frankly.

"Ah! Wait, one moment. You see I have had so many affairs! First, let me fix in my mind the circumstances of this particular case ... Ah! yes, now I have it. The Cahorn affair, Malaquis castle, Seine-Inférieure ... Two Rubens, a Watteau, and a few trifling articles."

"Trifling!"

"Oh! Ma foi, all that is of slight importance. But it suffices to know that the affair interests you. How can I serve you, Ganimard?"

"Must I explain to you what steps the authorities have taken in the matter?"

"Not at all. I have read the newspapers and I will frankly state that you have made very little progress."

"And that is the reason I have come to see you."

"I am entirely at your service."

"In the first place, the Cahorn affair was managed by you?"

"From A to Z."

"The letter of warning? the telegram?"

"All mine. I ought to have the receipts somewhere."

Arsène opened the drawer of a small table of plain white wood which, with the bed and stool, constituted all the furniture in his cell, and took therefrom two scraps of paper which he handed to Ganimard.

"Ah!" exclaimed the detective, in surprise, "I thought

you were closely guarded and searched, and I find that you read the newspapers and collect postal receipts."

"Bah! these people are so stupid! They open the lining of my vest, they examine the soles of my shoes, they sound the walls of my cell, but they never imagine that Arsène Lupin would be foolish enough to choose such a simple hiding place."

Ganimard laughed, as he said:

"What a droll fellow you are! Really, you bewilder me. But, come now, tell me about the Cahorn affair."

"Oh! oh! not quite so fast! You would rob me of all my secrets; expose all my little tricks. That is a very serious matter."

"Was I wrong to count on your complaisance?"

"No, Ganimard, and since you insist—"

Arsène Lupin paced his cell two or three times, then, stopping before Ganimard, he asked:

"What do you think of my letter to the baron?"

"I think you were amusing yourself by playing to the gallery."

"Ah! Playing to the gallery! Come, Ganimard, I thought you knew me better. Do I, Arsène Lupin, ever waste my time on such puerilities? Would I have written that letter if I could have robbed the baron without writing to him? I want you to understand that the letter was indispensable; it was the motor that set the whole machine in motion. Now, let us discuss together a scheme for the robbery of the Malaquis castle. Are you willing?"

"Yes, proceed."

"Well, let us suppose a castle carefully closed and barricaded like that of the Baron Cahorn. Am I to abandon my scheme and renounce the treasures that I covet, upon the pretext that the castle which holds them is inaccessible?"

"Evidently not."

"Should I make an assault upon the castle at the head of a band of adventurers as they did in ancient times?"

"That would be foolish."

"Can I gain admittance by stealth or cunning?"

"Impossible."

"Then there is only one way open to me. I must have the owner of the castle invite me to it."

"That is surely an original method."

"And how easy! Let us suppose that one day the owner receives a letter warning him that a notorious burglar known as Arsène Lupin is plotting to rob him. What will he do?"

"Send a letter to the Procureur."

"Who will laugh at him, because the said Arsène Lupin is actually in prison. Then, in his anxiety and fear, the simple man will ask the assistance of the first-comer, will he not?"

"Very likely."

"And if he happens to read in a country newspaper that a celebrated detective is spending his vacation in a neighbouring town—"

"He will seek that detective."

"Of course. But, on the other hand, let us presume that, having foreseen that state of affairs, the said Arsène Lupin has requested one of his friends to visit Caudebec, make the acquaintance of the editor of the *Réveil*, a newspaper to which the baron is a subscriber, and let said editor understand that such person is the celebrated detective—then, what will happen?"

"The editor will announce in the *Réveil* the presence in Caudebec of said detective."

"Exactly; and one of two things will happen: either the fish – I mean Cahorn – will not bite, and nothing will happen; or, what is more likely, he will run and greedily swallow the bait. Thus, behold my Baron Cahorn imploring the assistance of one of my friends against me."

"Original, indeed!"

"Of course, the pseudo-detective at first refuses to give any assistance. On top of that comes the telegram from Arsène Lupin. The frightened baron rushes once more to my friend and offers him a definite sum of money for his services. My friend accepts and summons two members of our band, who, during the night, whilst Cahorn is under the watchful eye of his protector, removes certain articles by way of the window and lowers them with ropes into a nice little launch chartered for the occasion. Simple, isn't it?"

"Marvellous! Marvellous!" exclaimed Ganimard. "The boldness of the scheme and the ingenuity of all its details are beyond criticism. But who is the detective whose name and fame served as a magnet to attract the baron and draw him into your net?"

"There is only one name could do it – only one."

"And that is?"

"Arsène Lupin's personal enemy – the most illustrious Ganimard."

"I?"

"Yourself, Ganimard. And, really, it is very funny.

If you go there, and the baron decides to talk, you will find that it will be your duty to arrest yourself, just as you arrested me in America. Hein! the revenge is really amusing: I cause Ganimard to arrest Ganimard."

Arsène Lupin laughed heartily. The detective, greatly vexed, bit his lips; to him the joke was quite devoid of humour. The arrival of a prison guard gave Ganimard an opportunity to recover himself. The man brought Arsène Lupin's luncheon, furnished by a neighbouring restaurant. After depositing the tray upon the table, the guard retired. Lupin broke his bread, ate a few morsels, and continued:

"But, rest easy, my dear Ganimard, you will not go to Malaquis. I can tell you something that will astonish you: the Cahorn affair is on the point of being settled."

"Excuse me; I have just seen the Chief of the Sureté."

"What of that? Does Monsieur Dudouis know my business better than I do myself? You will learn that Ganimard – excuse me – that the pseudo-Ganimard still remains on very good terms with the baron. The latter has authorized him to negotiate a very delicate transaction with me, and, at the present moment, in consideration of a certain sum, it is probable that the baron has recovered possession of his pictures and other treasures. And on their return, he will withdraw his complaint. Thus, there is no longer any theft, and the law must abandon the case."

Ganimard regarded the prisoner with a bewildered air.

"And how do you know all that?"

"I have just received the telegram I was expecting."

"You have just received a telegram?"

"This very moment, my dear friend. Out of politeness, I did not wish to read it in your presence. But if you will permit me—"

"You are joking, Lupin."

"My dear friend, if you will be so kind as to break that egg, you will learn for yourself that I am not joking."

Mechanically, Ganimard obeyed, and cracked the egg-shell with the blade of a knife. He uttered a cry of surprise. The shell contained nothing but a small piece of blue paper. At the request of Arsène he unfolded it. It was a telegram, or rather a portion of a telegram from which the postmarks had been removed. It read as follows:

Contract closed. Hundred thousand balls delivered. All well.

"One hundred thousand balls?" said Ganimard.

"Yes, one hundred thousand francs. Very little, but then, you know, these are hard times ... And I have some heavy bills to meet. If you only knew my budget ... living in the city comes very high."

Ganimard arose. His ill humour had disappeared. He reflected for a moment, glancing over the whole affair in an effort to discover a weak point; then, in a tone and manner that betrayed his admiration of the prisoner, he said:

"Fortunately, we do not have a dozen such as you to deal with; if we did, we would have to close up shop."

Arsène Lupin assumed a modest air, as he replied:

"Bah! A person must have some diversion to occupy his leisure hours, especially when he is in prison."

"What!" exclaimed Ganimard, "your trial, your

defense, the examination – isn't that sufficient to occupy your mind?"

"No, because I have decided not to be present at my trial."

"Oh! Oh!"

Arsène Lupin repeated, positively:

"I shall not be present at my trial."

"Really!"

"Ah! My dear monsieur, do you suppose I am going to rot upon the wet straw? You insult me. Arsène Lupin remains in prison just as long as it pleases him, and not one minute more."

"Perhaps it would have been more prudent if you had avoided getting there," said the detective, ironically.

"Ah! Monsieur jests? Monsieur must remember that he had the honour to effect my arrest. Know then, my worthy friend, that no one, not even you, could have placed a hand upon me if a much more important event had not occupied my attention at that critical moment."

"You astonish me."

"A woman was looking at me, Ganimard, and I loved her. Do you fully understand what that means: to be under the eyes of a woman that one loves? I cared for nothing in the world but that. And that is why I am here."

"Permit me to say: you have been here a long time."

"In the first place, I wished to forget. Do not laugh; it was a delightful adventure and it is still a tender memory. Besides, I have been suffering from neurasthenia. Life is so feverish these days that it is necessary to take the 'rest cure' occasionally, and I find this spot a sovereign remedy for my tired nerves."

"Arsène Lupin, you are not a bad fellow, after all."

"Thank you," said Lupin. "Ganimard, this is Friday. On Wednesday next, at four o'clock in the afternoon, I will smoke my cigar at your house in the rue Pergolese."

"Arsène Lupin, I will expect you."

They shook hands like two old friends who valued each other at their true worth; then the detective stepped to the door.

"Ganimard!"

"What is it?" asked Ganimard, as he turned back.

"You have forgotten your watch."

"My watch?"

"Yes, it strayed into my pocket."

He returned the watch, excusing himself.

"Pardon me ... a bad habit. Because they have taken mine is no reason why I should take yours. Besides, I have a chronometer here that satisfies me fairly well."

He took from the drawer a large gold watch and heavy chain.

"From whose pocket did that come?" asked Ganimard.

Arsène Lupin gave a hasty glance at the initials engraved on the watch.

"J.B. ... Who the devil can that be? Ah! Yes, I remember. Jules Bouvier, the judge who conducted my examination. A charming fellow!"

THE ESCAPE OF ARSÈNE LUPIN

Arsène Lupin had just finished his repast and taken from his pocket an excellent cigar, with a gold band, which he was examining with unusual care, when the door of his cell was opened. He had barely time to throw the cigar into the drawer and move away from the table. The guard entered. It was the hour for exercise.

"I was waiting for you, my dear boy," exclaimed Lupin, in his accustomed good humour.

They went out together. As soon as they had disappeared at a turn in the corridor, two men entered the cell and commenced a minute examination of it. One was Inspector Dieuzy; the other was Inspector Folenfant. They wished to verify their suspicion that Arsène Lupin was in communication with his accomplices outside of the prison. On the preceding evening, the *Grand Journal* had published these lines addressed to its court reporter:

Monsieur:
In a recent article you referred to me in most unjustifiable

terms. Some days before the opening of my trial I will call you to account.

Arsène Lupin.

The handwriting was certainly that of Arsène Lupin. Consequently, he sent letters; and, no doubt, received letters. It was certain that he was preparing for that escape thus arrogantly announced by him.

The situation had become intolerable. Acting in conjunction with the examining judge, the chief of the Sûreté, Monsieur Dudouis, had visited the prison and instructed the gaoler in regard to the precautions necessary to ensure Lupin's safety. At the same time, he sent the two men to examine the prisoner's cell. They raised every stone, ransacked the bed, did everything customary in such a case, but they discovered nothing, and were about to abandon their investigation when the guard entered hastily and said:

"The drawer ... look in the table-drawer. When I entered just now, he was closing it."

They opened the drawer, and Dieuzy exclaimed:

"Ah! We have him this time."

Folenfant stopped him.

"Wait a moment. The chief will want to make an inventory."

"This is a very choice cigar."

"Leave it there, and notify the chief."

Two minutes later Monsieur Dudouis examined the contents of the drawer. First he discovered a bundle of newspaper clippings relating to Arsène Lupin taken from the *Argus de la Presse,* then a tobacco-box, a pipe, some paper called 'onion-peel', and two books. He read the titles of the books. One was an English edition of Carlyle's *Hero-worship*; the other was a charming elzevir, in modern binding, the *Manual of Epictetus*, a German translation published at Leyden in 1634. On examining the books, he found that all the pages were underlined and annotated. Were they prepared as a code for correspondence, or did they simply express the studious character of the reader? Then he examined the tobacco-box and the pipe. Finally, he took up the famous cigar with its gold band.

"Fichtre!" he exclaimed. "Our friend smokes a good cigar. It's a Henry Clay."

With the mechanical action of an habitual smoker, he placed the cigar close to his ear and squeezed it to make it crack. Immediately he uttered a cry of surprise. The cigar had yielded under the pressure of his fingers. He examined it more closely, and quickly discovered something white between the leaves of tobacco. Delicately, with the aid of a pin, he withdrew a roll of very thin paper, scarcely larger than a toothpick. It was a letter. He unrolled it, and found these words, written in a feminine handwriting:

The basket has taken the place of the others. Eight out of ten are ready. On pressing the outer foot the plate goes downward. From twelve to sixteen every day, H-P will wait. But where? Reply at once. Rest easy; your friend is watching over you.

Monsieur Dudouis reflected a moment, then said:
"It is quite clear ... the basket ... the eight compartments ...

From twelve to sixteen means from twelve to four o'clock."

"But this H-P, that will wait?"

"H-P must mean automobile. H-P, horsepower, is the way they indicate strength of the motor. A twenty-four H-P is an automobile of twenty-four horsepower."

Then he rose, and asked:

"Had the prisoner finished his breakfast?"

"Yes."

"And as he has not yet read the message, which is proved by the condition of the cigar, it is probable that he had just received it."

"How?"

"In his food. Concealed in his bread or in a potato, perhaps."

"Impossible. His food was allowed to be brought in simply to trap him, but we have never found anything in it."

"We will look for Lupin's reply this evening. Detain him outside for a few minutes. I shall take this to the examining judge, and, if he agrees with me, we will have the letter photographed at once, and in an hour you can replace the letter in the drawer in a cigar similar to this. The prisoner must have no cause for suspicion."

It was not without a certain curiosity that Monsieur Dudouis returned to the prison in the evening, accompanied by Inspector Dieuzy. Three empty plates were sitting on the stove in the corner.

"He has eaten?"

"Yes," replied the guard.

"Dieuzy, please cut that macaroni into very small pieces, and open that bread roll ... Nothing?"

"No, chief."

Monsieur Dudouis examined the plates, the fork, the spoon, and the knife – an ordinary knife with a rounded blade. He turned the handle to the left; then to the right. It yielded and unscrewed. The knife was hollow, and served as a hiding-place for a sheet of paper.

"Peuh!" he said, "that is not very clever for a man like Arsène. But we mustn't lose any time. You, Dieuzy, go and search the restaurant."

Then he read the note:

"I trust to you, H-P will follow at a distance every day. I will go ahead. Au revoir, dear friend."

"At last," cried Monsieur Dudouis, rubbing his hands gleefully, "I think we have the affair in our own hands. A little strategy on our part, and the escape will be a success in so far as the arrest of his confederates are concerned."

"But if Arsène Lupin slips through your fingers?" suggested the guard.

"We will have a sufficient number of men to prevent that. If, however, he displays too much cleverness, ma foi, so much the worse for him! As to his band of robbers, since the chief refuses to speak, the others must."

* * *

And, as a matter of fact, Arsène Lupin had very little to say. For several months, Monsieur Jules Bouvier, the examining judge, had exerted himself in vain. The investigation had been reduced to a few uninteresting arguments between the judge and the advocate, Maître Danval, one of the leaders of the bar. From time to time, through courtesy, Arsène Lupin would speak. One day he said:

"Yes, Monsieur Le Judge, I quite agree with you: the robbery of the Crédit Lyonnais, the theft in the rue de Babylone, the issue of the counterfeit banknotes, the burglaries at the various châteaux, Armesnil, Gouret, Imblevain, Groseillers, Malaquis, all my work, monsieur, I did it all."

"Then will you explain to me–"

"It is useless. I confess everything in a lump, everything and even ten times more than you know nothing about."

Wearied by his fruitless task, the judge had suspended his examinations, but he resumed them after the two intercepted messages were brought to his attention; and regularly, at midday, Arsène Lupin was taken from the prison to the Dépôt in the prison van with a certain number of other prisoners. They returned about three or four o'clock.

Now, one afternoon, this return trip was made under unusual conditions. The other prisoners not having been examined, it was decided to take back Arsène Lupin first, thus he found himself alone in the vehicle.

These prison vans, vulgarly called 'panniers à salade'– or salad baskets – are divided lengthwise by a central corridor from which open ten compartments, five on either side. Each compartment is so arranged that the occupant must assume and retain a sitting posture, and, consequently, the five prisoners are seated one upon the other, and yet separated one from the other by partitions. A municipal guard, standing at one end, watches over the corridor.

Arsène was placed in the third cell on the right, and the heavy vehicle started. He carefully calculated when they left the quai de l'Horloge, and when they passed the Palais de Justice. Then, about the centre of the bridge Saint Michel, with his outer foot, that is to say, his right foot, he pressed upon the metal plate that closed his cell. Immediately something clicked, and the metal plate moved. He was able to ascertain that he was located between the two wheels.

He waited, keeping a sharp lookout. The vehicle was proceeding slowly along the boulevard Saint Michel. At the corner of Saint Germain, it stopped. A truck horse had fallen. The traffic having been interrupted, a vast throng of fiacres and omnibuses had gathered there. Arsène Lupin looked out. Another prison van had stopped close to the one he occupied. He moved the plate still farther, put his foot on one of the spokes of the wheel and leaped to the ground. A coachman saw him, roared with laughter, then tried to raise an outcry, but his voice was lost in the noise of the traffic that had commenced to move again. Moreover, Arsène Lupin was already far away.

He had run for a few steps; but once upon the sidewalk, he turned and looked around; he seemed to scent the wind like a person who is uncertain which direction to take. Then, having decided, he put his hands in his pockets, and, with the careless air of an idle stroller, he proceeded up the boulevard. It was a warm, bright autumn day, and the cafés were full. He took a seat on the terrace of one of them. He ordered a bock and a package of cigarettes. He emptied his glass slowly, smoked one cigarette and lighted a second. Then he asked the waiter to send the proprietor to him. When the proprietor came, Arsène spoke to him in a voice loud enough to be heard by everyone:

"I regret to say, monsieur, I have forgotten my pocketbook. Perhaps, on the strength of my name, you will be pleased to give me credit for a few days. I am Arsène Lupin."

The proprietor looked at him, thinking he was joking. But Arsène repeated:

"Lupin, prisoner at the Santé, but now a fugitive. I venture to assume that the name inspires you with perfect confidence in me."

And he walked away, amidst shouts of laughter, whilst the proprietor stood amazed.

Lupin strolled along the rue Soufflot, and turned into the rue Saint Jacques. He pursued his way slowly, smoking his cigarettes and looking into the shop-windows. At the Boulevard de Port Royal he took his bearings, discovered where he was, and then walked in the direction of the rue de la Santé. The high forbidding walls of the prison were now before him. He pulled his hat forwards to shade his face; then, approaching the sentinel, he asked:

"Is this the prison de la Santé?"

"Yes."

"I wish to regain my cell. The van left me on the way, and I would not abuse–"

"Now, young man, move along – quick!" growled the sentinel.

"Pardon me, but I must pass through that gate. And if you prevent Arsène Lupin from entering the prison it will cost you dear, my friend."

"Arsène Lupin! What are you talking about!"

"I am sorry I haven't a card with me," said Arsène, fumbling in his pockets.

The sentinel eyed him from head to foot, in astonishment. Then, without a word, he rang a bell. The iron gate was partly opened, and Arsène stepped inside. Almost immediately he encountered the keeper of the prison, gesticulating and feigning a violent anger. Arsène smiled and said:

"Come, monsieur, don't play that game with me. What! They take the precaution to carry me alone in the van, prepare a nice little obstruction, and imagine I am going to take to my heels and rejoin my friends. Well, and what about the twenty agents of the Sûreté who accompanied us on foot, in fiacres and on bicycles? No, the arrangement did not please me. I should not have got away alive. Tell me, monsieur, did they count on that?"

He shrugged his shoulders, and added:

"I beg of you, monsieur, not to worry about me. When I wish to escape I shall not require any assistance."

On the second day thereafter, the *Echo de France*, which had apparently become the official reporter of the exploits of Arsène Lupin – it was said that he was one of its principal shareholders – published a most complete account of this attempted escape. The exact wording of the messages exchanged between the prisoner and his mysterious friend, the means by which correspondence was constructed, the complicity of the police, the promenade on the Boulevard Saint Michel, the incident at the café Soufflot, everything was disclosed. It was known that the search of the restaurant and its waiters by Inspector Dieuzy had been fruitless. And the public also learned an extraordinary thing which demonstrated the infinite variety of resources that Lupin possessed: the prison van, in which he was being carried, was prepared for the occasion and substituted by his accomplices for one of the six vans which did service at the prison.

The next escape of Arsène Lupin was not doubted by anyone. He announced it himself, in categorical terms, in a reply to Monsieur Bouvier on the day following his attempted escape. The judge having made a jest about the affair, Arsène was annoyed, and, firmly eyeing the judge, he said, emphatically:

"Listen to me, monsieur! I give you my word of honour that this attempted flight was simply preliminary to my general plan of escape."

"I do not understand," said the judge.

"It is not necessary that you should understand."

And when the judge, in the course of that examination which was reported at length in the columns of the *Echo de France,* when the judge sought to resume his investigation, Arsène Lupin exclaimed, with an assumed air of lassitude:

"Mon Dieu, Mon Dieu, what's the use! All these questions are of no importance!"

"What! No importance?" cried the judge.

"No; because I shall not be present at the trial."

"You will not be present?"

"No; I have fully decided on that, and nothing will change my mind."

Such assurance combined with the inexplicable indiscretions that Arsène committed every day served to annoy and mystify the officers of the law. There were secrets known only to Arsène Lupin; secrets that he alone could divulge. But for what purpose did he reveal them? And how?

Arsène Lupin was moved to another cell. The judge closed his preliminary investigation. No further proceedings were taken in his case for a period of two months, during which time Arsène was seen almost constantly lying on his bed with his face turned toward the wall. The changing of his cell seemed to discourage him. He refused to see his advocate. He exchanged only a few necessary words with his keepers.

During the fortnight preceding his trial, he resumed his vigorous life. He complained of want of air. Consequently, early every morning he was allowed to exercise in the courtyard, guarded by two men.

Public curiosity had not died out; every day it expected to be regaled with news of his escape; and, it is true, he had gained a considerable amount of public sympathy by reason of his verve, his gaiety, his diversity, his inventive genius and the mystery of his life. Arsène Lupin must escape. It was his inevitable fate. The public expected it, and was surprised that the event had been delayed so long. Every morning the Préfect of Police asked his secretary:

"Well, has he escaped yet?"

"No, Monsieur le Préfect."

"Tomorrow, probably."

And, on the day before the trial, a gentleman called at the office of the *Grand Journal,* asked to see the court reporter, threw his card in the reporter's face, and walked rapidly away. These words were written on the card: 'Arsène Lupin always keeps his promises.'

* * *

It was under these conditions that the trial commenced. An enormous crowd gathered at the court. Everybody wished to see the famous Arsène Lupin. They had a gleeful anticipation that the prisoner would play some audacious pranks upon the judge. Advocates and magistrates, reporters and men of the world, actresses and society women were crowded together on the benches provided for the public.

It was a dark, sombre day, with a steady downpour of rain. Only a dim light pervaded the courtroom, and the spectators caught a very indistinct view of the prisoner when the guards brought him in. But his heavy, shambling walk, the manner in which he dropped into his seat, and his passive, stupid appearance were not at all prepossessing. Several times his advocate – one of Monsieur Danval's assistants – spoke to him, but he simply shook his head and said nothing.

The clerk read the indictment, then the judge spoke:

"Prisoner at the bar, stand up. Your name, age, and occupation?"

Not receiving any reply, the judge repeated:

"Your name? I ask you your name?"

A thick, slow voice muttered:

"Baudru, Désiré."

A murmur of surprise pervaded the courtroom. But the judge proceeded:

"Baudru, Désiré? Ah! A new alias! Well, as you have already assumed a dozen different names and this one is, no doubt, as imaginary as the others, we will adhere to the name of Arsène Lupin, by which you are more generally known."

The judge referred to his notes, and continued:

"For, despite the most diligent search, your past history remains unknown. Your case is unique in the annals of crime. We know not whom you are, whence you came, your birth and breeding – all is a mystery to us. Three years ago you appeared in our midst as Arsène Lupin, presenting to us a strange combination of intelligence and perversion, immorality and generosity. Our knowledge of your life prior to that date is vague and problematical. It may be that the man called Rostat who, eight years ago, worked with Dickson, the prestidigitator, was none other than Arsène Lupin. It is probable that the Russian student who, six years ago, attended the laboratory of Doctor Altier at the Saint Louis Hospital, and who often astonished the doctor by the ingenuity of his hypotheses on subjects of bacteriology and the boldness of his experiments in diseases of the skin, was none other than Arsène Lupin. It is probable, also, that Arsène Lupin was the professor who introduced the Japanese art of ju-jitsu to the Parisian public. We have some reason to believe that Arsène Lupin was the bicyclist who won the Grand Prix de l'Exposition, received his ten thousand francs, and was never heard of again. Arsène Lupin may have been, also, the person who saved so many lives through the little dormer-window at the Charity Bazaar; and, at the same time, picked their pockets."

The judge paused for a moment, then continued:

"Such is that epoch which seems to have been utilized by you in a thorough preparation for the warfare you have since waged against society; a methodical apprenticeship in which you developed your strength, energy and skill to the highest point possible. Do you acknowledge the accuracy of these facts?"

During this discourse the prisoner had stood balancing himself, first on one foot, then on the other, with shoulders stooped and arms inert. Under the strongest light one could observe his extreme thinness, his hollow cheeks, his projecting cheek-bones, his earthen-coloured face dotted with small red spots and framed in a rough, straggling beard. Prison life had caused him to age and wither. He had lost the youthful face and elegant figure we had seen portrayed so often in the newspapers.

It appeared as if he had not heard the question propounded by the judge. Twice it was repeated to him. Then he raised his eyes, seemed to reflect, then, making a desperate effort, he murmured:

"Baudru, Désiré."

The judge smiled, as he said:

"I do not understand the theory of your defense, Arsène Lupin. If you are seeking to avoid responsibility for your crimes on the ground of imbecility, such a line of defense is open to you. But I shall proceed with the trial and pay no heed to your vagaries."

He then narrated at length the various thefts, swindles and forgeries charged against Lupin. Sometimes he questioned the prisoner, but the latter simply grunted or remained silent. The examination of witnesses commenced. Some of the evidence given was immaterial; other portions of it seemed more important, but through all of it there ran a vein of contradictions and inconsistencies. A wearisome obscurity enveloped the proceedings, until Detective Ganimard was called as a witness; then interest was revived.

From the beginning the actions of the veteran detective appeared strange and unaccountable. He was nervous and ill at ease. Several times he looked at the prisoner, with obvious doubt and anxiety. Then, with his hands resting on the rail in front of him, he recounted the events in which he had participated, including his pursuit of the prisoner across Europe and his arrival in America. He was listened to with great avidity, as his capture of Arsène Lupin was well known to everyone through the medium of the press. Toward the close of his testimony, after referring to his conversations with Arsène Lupin, he stopped twice, embarrassed and undecided. It was apparent that he was possessed of some thought which he feared to utter. The judge said to him, sympathetically:

"If you are ill, you may retire for the present."

"No, no, but–"

He stopped, looked sharply at the prisoner, and said:

"I ask permission to scrutinize the prisoner at closer range. There is some mystery about him that I must solve."

He approached the accused man, examined him attentively for several minutes, then returned to the witness-stand, and, in an almost solemn voice, he said:

"I declare, on oath, that the prisoner now before me is not Arsène Lupin."

A profound silence followed the statement. The judge, nonplussed for a moment, exclaimed:

"Ah! What do you mean? That is absurd!"

The detective continued:

"At first sight there is a certain resemblance, but if you carefully consider the nose, the mouth, the hair, the colour of skin, you will see that it is not Arsène Lupin. And the eyes! Did he ever have those alcoholic eyes!"

"Come, come, witness! What do you mean? Do you pretend to say that we are trying the wrong man?"

"In my opinion, yes. Arsène Lupin has, in some manner, contrived to put this poor devil in his place, unless this man is a willing accomplice."

This dramatic dénouement caused much laughter and excitement amongst the spectators. The judge adjourned the trial, and sent for Monsieur Bouvier, the gaoler, and guards employed in the prison.

When the trial was resumed, Monsieur Bouvier and the gaoler examined the accused and declared that there was only a very slight resemblance between the prisoner and Arsène Lupin.

"Well, then!" exclaimed the judge, "who is this man? Where does he come from? What is he in prison for?"

Two of the prison guards were called and both of them declared that the prisoner was Arsène Lupin. The judged breathed once more.

But one of the guards then said:

"Yes, yes, I think it is he."

"What!" cried the judge, impatiently, "you *think* it is he! What do you mean by that?"

"Well, I saw very little of the prisoner. He was placed

in my charge in the evening and, for two months, he seldom stirred, but laid on his bed with his face to the wall."

"What about the time prior to those two months?"

"Before that he occupied a cell in another part of the prison. He was not in cell 24."

Here the head gaoler interrupted, and said:

"We moved him to another cell after his attempted escape."

"But you, monsieur, you have seen him during those two months?"

"I had no occasion to see him. He was always quiet and orderly."

"And this prisoner is not Arsène Lupin?"

"No."

"Then who is he?" demanded the judge.

"I do not know."

"Then we have before us a man who was substituted for Arsène Lupin, two months ago. How do you explain that?"

"I cannot."

In absolute despair, the judge turned to the accused and addressed him in a conciliatory tone:

"Prisoner, can you tell me how, and since when, you became an inmate of the Prison de la Santé?"

The engaging manner of the judge was calculated to disarm the mistrust and awaken the understanding of the accused man. He tried to reply. Finally, under clever and gentle questioning, he succeeded in framing a few phrases from which the following story was gleaned: Two months ago, he had been taken to the Dépôt, examined and released. As he was leaving the building, a free man, he was seized by two guards and placed in the prison van. Since then he had occupied cell 24. He was contented there, plenty to eat, and he slept well – so he did not complain.

All that seemed probable; and, amidst the mirth and excitement of the spectators, the judge adjourned the trial until the story could be investigated and verified.

* * *

The following facts were at once established by an examination of the prison records: Eight weeks before a man named Baudru Désiré had slept at the Dépôt. He was released the next day, and left the Dépôt at two o'clock in the afternoon. On the same day at two o'clock, having been examined for the last time, Arsène Lupin left the Dépôt in a prison van.

Had the guards made a mistake? Had they been deceived by the resemblance and carelessly substituted this man for their prisoner?

Another question suggested itself: had the substitution been arranged in advance? In that event Baudru must have been an accomplice and must have caused his own arrest for the express purpose of taking Lupin's place. But then, by what miracle had such a plan, based on a series of improbable chances, been carried to success?

Baudru Désiré was turned over to the anthropological service; they had never seen anything like him. However, they easily traced his past history. He was known at Courbevois, at Asnières and at Levallois. He lived on alms and slept in one of those rag-picker's huts near the barrier de Ternes. He had disappeared from there a year ago.

Had he been enticed away by Arsène Lupin? There was no evidence to that effect. And even if that was so, it did not explain the flight of the prisoner. That still remained a mystery. Amongst twenty theories which sought to explain it, not one was satisfactory. Of the escape itself, there was no doubt; an escape that was incomprehensible, sensational, in which the public, as well as the officers of the law, could detect a carefully prepared plan, a combination of circumstances marvellously dove-tailed, whereof the dénouement fully justified the confident prediction of Arsène Lupin: 'I shall not be present at my trial.'

After a month of patient investigation, the problem remained unsolved. The poor devil of a Baudru could not be kept in prison indefinitely, and to place him on trial would be ridiculous. There was no charge against him. Consequently, he was released; but the chief of the Sûreté resolved to keep him under surveillance. This idea originated with Ganimard. From his point of view there was neither complicity nor chance. Baudru was an instrument upon which Arsène Lupin had played with his extraordinary skill. Baudru, when set at liberty, would lead them to Arsène Lupin or, at least, to some of his accomplices. The two inspectors, Folenfant and Dieuzy, were assigned to assist Ganimard.

One foggy morning in January the prison gates opened and Baudru Désiré stepped forth – a free man. At first he appeared to be quite embarrassed, and walked like a person who has no precise idea whither he is going.

He followed the rue de la Santé and the rue Saint Jacques. He stopped in front of an old-clothes shop, removed his jacket and his vest, sold his vest on which he realized a few sous; then, replacing his jacket, he proceeded on his way. He crossed the Seine. At the Châtelet an omnibus passed him. He wished to enter it, but there was no place. The controller advised him to secure a number, so he entered the waiting-room.

Ganimard called to his two assistants, and, without removing his eyes from the waiting room, he said to them:

"Stop a carriage ... no, two. That will be better. I will go with one of you, and we will follow him."

The men obeyed. Yet Baudru did not appear. Ganimard entered the waiting-room. It was empty.

"Idiot that I am!" he muttered, "I forgot there was another exit."

There was an interior corridor extending from the waiting room to the rue Saint Martin. Ganimard rushed through it and arrived just in time to observe Baudru upon the top of the Batignolles-Jardin de Plates omnibus as it was turning the corner of the rue de Rivoli. He ran and caught the omnibus. But he had lost his two assistants. He must continue the pursuit alone. In his anger he was inclined to seize the man by the collar without ceremony. Was it not with premeditation and by means of an ingenious ruse that his pretended imbecile had separated him from his assistants?

He looked at Baudru. The latter was asleep on the bench, his head rolling from side to side, his mouth half-opened, and an incredible expression of stupidity on his blotched face. No, such an adversary was incapable of deceiving old

Ganimard. It was a stroke of luck – nothing more.

At the Galleries-Lafayette, the man leaped from the omnibus and took the La Muette tramway, following the boulevard Haussmann and the avenue Victor Hugo. Baudru alighted at La Muette station; and, with a nonchalant air, strolled into the Bois de Boulogne.

He wandered through one path after another, and sometimes retraced his steps. What was he seeking? Had he any definite object? At the end of an hour, he appeared to be faint from fatigue, and, noticing a bench, he sat down. The spot, not far from Auteuil, on the edge of a pond hidden amongst the trees, was absolutely deserted. After the lapse of another half-hour, Ganimard became impatient and resolved to speak to the man. He approached and took a seat beside Baudru, lighted a cigarette, traced some figures in the sand with the end of his cane, and said:

"It's a pleasant day."

No response. But, suddenly the man burst into laughter, a happy, mirthful laugh, spontaneous and irresistible. Ganimard felt his hair stand on end in horror and surprise. It was that laugh, that infernal laugh he knew so well!

With a sudden movement, he seized the man by the collar and looked at him with a keen, penetrating gaze; and found that he no longer saw the man Baudru. To be sure, he saw Baudru; but, at the same time, he saw the other, the real man, Lupin. He discovered the intense life in the eyes, he filled up the shrunken features, he perceived the real flesh beneath the flabby skin, the real mouth through the grimaces that deformed it. Those were the eyes and mouth of the other, and especially his keen, alert, mocking expression, so clear and youthful!

"Arsène Lupin, Arsène Lupin," he stammered.

Then, in a sudden fit of rage, he seized Lupin by the throat and tried to hold him down. In spite of his fifty years, he still possessed unusual strength, whilst his adversary was apparently in a weak condition. But the struggle was a brief one. Arsène Lupin made only a slight movement, and, as suddenly as he had made the attack, Ganimard released his hold. His right arm fell inert, useless.

"If you had taken lessons in jiu-jitsu at the quai des Orfèvres," said Lupin, "you would know that that blow is called udi-shi-ghi in Japanese. A second more, and I would have broken your arm and that would have been just what you deserve. I am surprised that you, an old friend whom I respect and before whom I voluntarily expose my incognito, should abuse my confidence in that violent manner. It is unworthy – Ah! What's the matter?"

Ganimard did not reply. That escape for which he deemed himself responsible – was it not he, Ganimard, who, by his sensational evidence, had led the court into serious error? That escape appeared to him like a dark cloud on his professional career. A tear rolled down his cheek to his grey moustache.

"Oh! mon Dieu, Ganimard, don't take it to heart. If you had not spoken, I would have arranged for someone else to do it. I couldn't allow poor Baudru Désiré to be convicted."

"Then," murmured Ganimard, "it was you that was there? And now you are here?"

"It is I, always I, only I."

"Can it be possible?"

"Oh, it is not the work of a sorcerer. Simply, as the judge remarked at the trial, the apprenticeship of a dozen years that equips a man to cope successfully with all the obstacles in life."

"But your face? Your eyes?"

"You can understand that if I worked eighteen months with Doctor Altier at the Saint-Louis hospital, it was not out of love for the work. I considered that he, who would one day have the honour of calling himself Arsène Lupin, ought to be exempt from the ordinary laws governing appearance and identity. Appearance? That can be modified at will. For instance, a hypodermic injection of paraffine will puff up the skin at the desired spot. Pyrogallic acid will change your skin to that of an Indian. The juice of the greater celandine will adorn you with the most beautiful eruptions and tumours. Another chemical affects the growth of your beard and hair; another changes the tone of your voice. Add to that two months of dieting in cell 24; exercises repeated a thousand times to enable me to hold my features in a certain grimace, to carry my head at a certain inclination, and adapt my back and shoulders to a stooping posture. Then five drops of atropine in the eyes to make them haggard and wild, and the trick is done."

"I do not understand how you deceived the guards."

"The change was progressive. The evolution was so gradual that they failed to notice it."

"But Baudru Désiré?"

"Baudru exists. He is a poor, harmless fellow whom I

met last year; and, really, he bears a certain resemblance to me. Considering my arrest as a possible event, I took charge of Baudru and studied the points wherein we differed in appearance with a view to correct them in my own person. My friends caused him to remain at the Dépôt overnight, and to leave there next day about the same hour as I did – a coincidence easily arranged. Of course, it was necessary to have a record of his detention at the Dépôt in order to establish the fact that such a person was a reality; otherwise, the police would have sought elsewhere to find out my identity. But, in offering to them this excellent Baudru, it was inevitable, you understand, inevitable that they would seize upon him, and, despite the insurmountable difficulties of a substitution, they would prefer to believe in a substitution than confess their ignorance."

"Yes, yes, of course," said Ganimard.

"And then," exclaimed Arsène Lupin, "I held in my hands a trump card: an anxious public watching and waiting for my escape. And that is the fatal error into which you fell, you and the others, in the course of that fascinating game pending between me and the officers of the law wherein the stake was my liberty. And you supposed that I was playing to the gallery; that I was intoxicated with my success. I, Arsène Lupin, guilty of such weakness! Oh, no! And, no longer ago than the Cahorn affair, you said: 'When Arsène Lupin cries from the housetops that he will escape, he has some object in view.' But, sapristi, you must understand that in order to escape I must create in advance a public belief in that escape, a belief amounting to an article of faith, an absolute conviction, a reality as glittering as the sun. And I did create that belief that Arsène Lupin would escape, that Arsène Lupin would not be present at his trial. And when you gave your evidence and said: 'That man is not Arsène Lupin,' everybody was prepared to believe you. Had one person doubted it, had any one uttered this simple restriction: Suppose it is Arsène Lupin? – from that moment, I was lost. If anyone had scrutinized my face, not imbued with the idea that I was not Arsène Lupin, as you and the others did at my trial, but with the idea that I might be Arsène Lupin; then, despite all my precautions, I should have been recognized. But I had no fear. Logically, psychologically, no one could entertain the idea that I was Arsène Lupin."

He grasped Ganimard's hand.

"Come, Ganimard, confess that on the Wednesday after our conversation in the prison de la Santé, you expected me at your house at four o'clock, exactly as I said I would go."

"And your prison van?" said Ganimard, evading the question.

"A bluff! Some of my friends secured that old unused van and wished to make the attempt. But I considered it impractical without the concurrence of a number of unusual circumstances. However, I found it useful to carry out that attempted escape and give it the widest publicity. An audaciously planned escape, though not completed, gave to the succeeding one the character of reality simply by anticipation."

"So that the cigar ..."

"Hollowed by myself, as well as the knife."

"And the letters?"

"Written by me."

"And the mysterious correspondent?"

"Did not exist."

Ganimard reflected a moment, then said:

"When the anthropological service had Baudru's case under consideration, why did they not perceive that his measurements coincided with those of Arsène Lupin?"

"My measurements are not in existence."

"Indeed!"

"At least, they are false. I have given considerable attention to that question. In the first place, the Bertillon system records the visible marks of identification – and you have seen that they are not infallible – and, after that, the measurements of the head, the fingers, the ears, etc. Of course, such measurements are more or less infallible."

"Absolutely."

"No; but it costs money to get around them. Before we left America, one of the employees of the service there accepted so much money to insert false figures in my measurements. Consequently, Baudru's measurements should not agree with those of Arsène Lupin."

After a short silence, Ganimard asked:

"What are you going to do now?"

"Now," replied Lupin, "I am going to take a rest, enjoy the best of food and drink and gradually recover my former healthy condition. It is all very well to become Baudru or some other person, on occasion, and to change your personality as you do your shirt, but you soon grow weary of the change. I feel exactly as I imagine the man who lost his shadow must have felt, and I shall be glad to be Arsène Lupin once more."

He walked to and fro for a few minutes, then, stopping in front of Ganimard, he said:

"You have nothing more to say, I suppose?"

"Yes. I should like to know if you intend to reveal the true state of facts connected with your escape. The mistake that I made–"

"Oh! No one will ever know that it was Arsène Lupin who was discharged. It is to my own interest to surround myself with mystery, and therefore I shall permit my escape to retain its almost miraculous character. So, have no fear on that score, my dear friend. I shall say nothing. And now, goodbye. I am going out to dinner this evening, and have only sufficient time to dress."

"I though you wanted a rest."

"Ah! there are duties to society that one cannot avoid. Tomorrow, I shall rest."

"Where do you dine tonight?"

"With the British Ambassador!"

THE MYSTERIOUS TRAVELLER

The evening before, I had sent my automobile to Rouen by the highway. I was to travel to Rouen by rail, on my way to visit some friends that live on the banks of the Seine.

At Paris, a few minutes before the train started, seven gentlemen entered my compartment; five of them were smoking. No matter that the journey was a short one, the thought of travelling with such a company was not agreeable to me, especially as the car was built on the old model, without a corridor. I picked up my overcoat, my newspapers and my timetable, and sought refuge in a neighbouring compartment.

It was occupied by a lady who, at sight of me, made a gesture of annoyance that did not escape my notice, and she leaned toward a gentleman who was standing on the step and was, no doubt, her husband. The gentleman scrutinized me closely, and apparently my appearance did not displease him, for he smiled as he spoke to his wife with the air of one who reassures a frightened child.

She smiled also, and gave me a friendly glance as if she now understood that I was one of those gallant men with whom a woman can remain shut up for two hours in a little box, six feet square, and have nothing to fear.

Her husband said to her:

"I have an important appointment, my dear, and cannot wait any longer. Adieu."

He kissed her affectionately and went away. His wife threw him a few kisses and waved her handkerchief. The whistle sounded, and the train started.

At that precise moment, and despite the protests of the guards, the door was opened, and a man rushed into our compartment. My companion, who was standing and arranging her luggage, uttered a cry of terror and fell upon the seat. I am not a coward – far from it – but I confess that such intrusions at the last minute are always disconcerting. They have a suspicious, unnatural aspect.

However, the appearance of the new arrival greatly modified the unfavourable impression produced by his precipitant action. He was correctly and elegantly dressed, wore a tasteful cravat, correct gloves, and his face was refined and intelligent. But, where the devil had I seen that face before? Because, beyond all possible doubt, I had seen it. And yet the memory of it was so vague and indistinct that I felt it would be useless to try to recall it at that time.

Then, directing my attention to the lady, I was amazed at the pallor and anxiety I saw in her face. She was looking at her neighbour – they occupied seats on the same side of the compartment – with an expression of intense alarm, and I perceived that one of her trembling hands was slowly gliding toward a little travelling bag that was lying on the seat about twenty inches from her. She finished by seizing it and nervously drawing it to her. Our eyes met, and I read in hers so much anxiety and fear that I could not refrain from speaking to her:

"Are you ill, madame? Shall I open the window?"

Her only reply was a gesture indicating that she was afraid of our companion. I smiled, as her husband had done, shrugged my shoulders, and explained to her, in pantomime, that she had nothing to fear, that I was there, and, besides, the gentleman appeared to be a very harmless individual. At that moment, he turned toward us, scrutinized both of us from head to foot, then settled down in his corner and paid us no more attention.

After a short silence, the lady, as if she had mustered all her energy to perform a desperate act, said to me, in an almost inaudible voice:

"Do you know who is on our train?"

"Who?"

"He ... he ...I assure you ..."

"Who is he?"

"Arsène Lupin!"

She had not taken her eyes off our companion, and it was to him rather than to me that she uttered the syllables of that disquieting name. He drew his hat over his face. Was that to conceal his agitation or, simply, to arrange himself for sleep? Then I said to her:

"Yesterday, through contumacy, Arsène Lupin was sentenced to twenty years' imprisonment at hard labour. Therefore it is improbable that he would be so imprudent, today, as to show himself in public. Moreover, the newspapers have announced his appearance in Turkey since his escape from the Santé."

"But he is on this train at the present moment," the lady proclaimed, with the obvious intention of being heard by our companion; "my husband is one of the directors in the penitentiary service, and it was the stationmaster himself who told us that a search being made for Arsène Lupin."

"They may have been mistaken–"

"No; he was seen in the waiting room. He bought a first-class ticket for Rouen."

"He has disappeared. The guard at the waiting-room door did not see him pass, and it is supposed that he had got into the express that leaves ten minutes after us."

"In that case, they will be sure to catch him."

"Unless, at the last moment, he leaped from that train to come here, into our train ... which is quite probable ... which is almost certain."

"If so, he will be arrested just the same; for the employees and guards would no doubt observe his passage from one train to the other, and, when we arrive at Rouen, they will arrest him there."

"Him – never! He will find some means of escape."

"In that case, I wish him 'bon voyage'."

"But, in the meantime, think what he may do!"

"What?"

"I don't know. He may do anything."

She was greatly agitated, and, truly, the situation justified, to some extent, her nervous excitement. I was impelled to say to her:

"Of course, there are many strange coincidences, but

you need have no fear. Admitting that Arsène Lupin is on this train, he will not commit any indiscretion; he will be only too happy to escape the peril that already threatens him."

My words did not reassure her, but she remained silent for a time. I unfolded my newspapers and read reports of Arsène Lupin's trial, but, as they contained nothing that was new to me, I was not greatly interested. Moreover, I was tired and sleepy. I felt my eyelids close and my head drop.

"But, monsieur, you are not going to sleep!"

She seized my newspaper, and looked at me with indignation.

"Certainly not," I said.

"That would be very imprudent."

"Of course," I assented.

I struggled to keep awake. I looked through the window at the landscape and the fleeting clouds, but in a short time all that became confused and indistinct; the image of the nervous lady and the drowsy gentleman were effaced from my memory, and I was buried in the soothing depths of a profound sleep. The tranquillity of my response was soon disturbed by disquieting dreams, wherein a creature that had played the part and bore the name of Arsène Lupin held an important place. He appeared to me with his back laden with articles of value; he leaped over walls, and plundered castles. But the outlines of that creature, who was no longer Arsène Lupin, assumed a more definite form. He came toward me, growing larger and larger, leaped into the compartment with incredible agility, and landed squarely on my chest. With a cry of fright and pain, I awoke. The man, the traveller, our companion, with his knee on my breast, held me by the throat.

My sight was very indistinct, for my eyes were suffused with blood. I could see the lady, in a corner of the compartment, convulsed with fright. I tried even not to resist. Besides, I did not have the strength. My temples throbbed; I was almost strangled. One minute more, and I would have breathed my last. The man must have realized it, for he relaxed his grip, but did not remove his hand. Then he took a cord, in which he had prepared a slip-knot, and tied my wrists together. In an instant, I was bound, gagged, and helpless.

Certainly, he accomplished the trick with an ease and skill that revealed the hand of a master; he was, no doubt, a professional thief. Not a word, not a nervous movement; only coolness and audacity. And I was there, lying on the bench, bound like a mummy, I – Arsène Lupin!

It was anything but a laughing matter, and yet, despite the gravity of the situation, I keenly appreciated the humour and irony that it involved. Arsène Lupin seized and bound like a novice! Robbed as if I were an unsophisticated rustic – for, you must understand, the scoundrel had deprived me of my purse and wallet! Arsène Lupin, a victim, duped, vanquished ... What an adventure!

The lady did not move. He did not even notice her. He contented himself with picking up her travelling-bag that had fallen to the floor and taking from it the jewels, purse, and gold and silver trinkets that it contained.

The lady opened her eyes, trembled with fear, drew the rings from her fingers and handed them to the man as if she wished to spare him unnecessary trouble. He took the rings and looked at her. She swooned.

Then, quite unruffled, he resumed his seat, lighted a cigarette, and proceeded to examine the treasure that he had acquired. The examination appeared to give him perfect satisfaction.

But I was not so well satisfied. I do not speak of the twelve thousand francs of which I had been unduly deprived: that was only a temporary loss, because I was certain that I would recover possession of that money after a very brief delay, together with the important papers contained in my wallet: plans, specifications, addresses, lists of correspondents, and compromising letters. But, for the moment, a more immediate and more serious question troubled me: How would this affair end? What would be the outcome of this adventure?

As you can imagine, the disturbance created by my passage through the Saint-Lazare station has not escaped my notice. Going to visit friends who knew me under the name of Guillaume Berlat, and amongst whom my resemblance to Arsène Lupin was a subject of many innocent jests, I could not assume a disguise, and my presence had been noticed. So, beyond question, the commissary of police at Rouen, notified by telegraph, and assisted by numerous agents, would be awaiting the train, would question all suspicious passengers, and proceed to search the cars.

Of course, I had foreseen all that, but it had not disturbed me, as I was certain that the police of Rouen would not be any shrewder than the police of Paris and that I could escape recognition; would it not be sufficient for me to carelessly display my card as 'député,' thanks to which I had inspired complete confidence in the gate-keeper at Saint-Lazare? – But the situation was greatly changed. I was no longer free. It was impossible to attempt one of my usual tricks. In one of the compartments, the commissary of police would find Monsieur Arsène Lupin, bound hand and foot, as docile as a lamb, packed up, all ready to be dumped into a prison van. He would have simply to accept delivery of the parcel, the same as if it were so much merchandise or a basket of fruit and vegetables. Yet, to avoid that shameful dénouement, what could I do – bound and gagged, as I was? And the train was rushing on toward Rouen, the next and only station.

Another problem was presented, in which I was less interested, but the solution of which aroused my professional curiosity. What were the intentions of my rascally companion? Of course, if I had been alone, he could, on our arrival at Rouen, leave the car slowly and fearlessly. But the lady? As soon as the door of the compartment should be opened, the lady, now so quiet and humble, would scream and call for help. That was the dilemma that perplexed me! Why had he not reduced her to a helpless condition similar to mine? That would have given him ample time to disappear before his double crime was discovered.

He was still smoking, with his eyes fixed upon the window that was now being streaked with drops of rain. Once he turned, picked up my timetable, and consulted it.

The lady had to feign a continued lack of consciousness in order to deceive the enemy. But fits of coughing, provoked by the smoke, exposed her true condition. As to me, I was very uncomfortable, and very tired. And I meditated; I plotted.

The train was rushing on, joyously, intoxicated with its own speed.

Saint Etienne ...! At that moment, the man arose and took two steps toward us, which caused the lady to utter a cry of alarm and fall into a genuine swoon. What was the man about to do? He lowered the window on our side. A heavy rain was now falling, and, by a gesture, the man expressed his annoyance at his not having an umbrella or an overcoat. He glanced at the rack. The lady's umbrella was there. He took it. He also took my overcoat and put it on.

We were now crossing the Seine. He turned up the bottoms of his trousers, then leaned over and raised the exterior latch of the door. Was he going to throw himself upon the track? At that speed, it would have been instant death. We now entered a tunnel. The man opened the door half-way and stood on the upper step. What folly! The darkness, the smoke, the noise, all gave a fantastic appearance to his actions. But suddenly, the train diminished its speed. A moment later it increased its speed, then slowed up again. Probably, some repairs were being made in that part of the tunnel which obliged the trains to diminish their speed, and the man was aware of the fact. He immediately stepped down to the lower step, closed the door behind him, and leaped to the ground. He was gone.

The lady immediately recovered her wits, and her first act was to lament the loss of her jewels. I gave her an imploring look. She understood, and quickly removed the gag that stifled me. She wished to untie the cords that bound me, but I prevented her.

"No, no, the police must see everything exactly as it stands. I want them to see what the rascal did to us."

"Suppose I pull the alarm-bell?"

"Too late. You should have done that when he made the attack on me."

"But he would have killed me. Ah! monsieur, didn't I tell you that he was on this train. I recognized him from his portrait. And now he has gone off with my jewels."

"Don't worry. The police will catch him."

"Catch Arsène Lupin! Never."

"That depends on you, madame. Listen. When we arrive at Rouen, be at the door and call. Make a noise. The police and the railway employees will come. Tell what you have seen: the assault made on me and the flight of Arsène Lupin. Give a description of him – soft hat, umbrella – yours – grey overcoat ..."

"Yours," said she.

"What! Mine? Not at all. It was his. I didn't have any."

"It seems to me he didn't have one when he came in."

"Yes, yes ... unless the coat was one that someone had forgotten and left in the rack. At all events, he had it when he went away, and that is the essential point. A grey overcoat – remember ... Ah! I forgot. You must tell your name, first thing you do. Your husband's official position will stimulate the zeal of the police."

We arrived at the station. I gave her some further instructions in a rather imperious tone:

"Tell them my name – Guillaume Berlat. If necessary, say that you know me. That will save time. We must expedite the preliminary investigation. The important thing is the pursuit of Arsène Lupin. Your jewels, remember! Let there be no mistake. Guillaume Berlat, a friend of your husband."

"I understand ... Guillaume Berlat."

She was already calling and gesticulating. As soon as the train stopped, several men entered the compartment. The critical moment had come.

Panting for breath, the lady exclaimed:

"Arsène Lupin ... he attacked us ... he stole my jewels ... I am Madame Renaud ... my husband is a director of the penitentiary service ... Ah! Here is my brother, Georges Ardelle, director of the Crédit Rouennais ... you must know ..."

She embraced a young man who had just joined us, and whom the commissary saluted. Then she continued, weeping:

"Yes, Arsène Lupin ... while monsieur was sleeping, he seized him by the throat ... Monsieur Berlat, a friend of my husband."

The commissary asked:

"But where is Arsène Lupin?"

"He leaped from the train, when passing through the tunnel."

"Are you sure that it was he?"

"Am I sure! I recognized him perfectly. Besides, he was seen at the Saint-Lazare station. He wore a soft hat–"

"No, a hard felt, like that," said the commissary, pointing to my hat.

"He had a soft hat, I am sure," repeated Madame Renaud, "and a grey overcoat."

"Yes, that is right," replied the commissary, "the telegram says he wore a grey overcoat with a black velvet collar."

"Exactly, a black velvet collar," exclaimed Madame Renaud, triumphantly.

I breathed freely. Ah! The excellent friend I had in that little woman.

The police agents had now released me. I bit my lips until they ran blood. Stooping over, with my handkerchief over my mouth, an attitude quite natural in a person who has remained for a long time in an uncomfortable position, and whose mouth shows the bloody marks of the gag, I addressed the commissary, in a weak voice:

"Monsieur, it was Arsène Lupin. There is no doubt about that. If we make haste, he can be caught yet. I think I may be of some service to you."

The railway car, in which the crime occurred, was detached from the train to serve as a mute witness at the official investigation. The train continued on its way to Havre. We were then conducted to the stationmaster's office through a crowd of curious spectators.

Then, I had a sudden access of doubt and discretion. Under some pretext or other, I must gain my automobile, and escape. To remain there was dangerous. Something might happen; for instance, a telegram from Paris, and I would be lost.

Yes, but what about my thief? Abandoned to my own resources, in an unfamiliar country, I could not hope to catch him.

"Bah! I must make the attempt," I said to myself. "It may be a difficult game, but an amusing one, and the stake is well worth the trouble."

And when the commissary asked us to repeat the story of the robbery, I exclaimed:

"Monsieur, really, Arsène Lupin is getting the start of us. My automobile is waiting in the courtyard. If you will be so kind as to use it, we can try ..."

The commissary smiled, and replied:

"The idea is a good one; so good, indeed, that it is already being carried out. Two of my men have set out on bicycles. They have been gone for some time."

"Where did they go?"

"To the entrance of the tunnel. There, they will gather evidence, secure witnesses, and follow on the track of Arsène Lupin."

I could not refrain from shrugging my shoulders, as I replied:

"Your men will not secure any evidence or any witnesses."

"Really!"

"Arsène Lupin will not allow anyone to see him emerge from the tunnel. He will take the first road—"

"To Rouen, where we will arrest him."

"He will not go to Rouen."

"Then he will remain in the vicinity, where his capture will be even more certain."

"He will not remain in the vicinity."

"Oh! Oh! And where will he hide?"

I looked at my watch, and said:

"At the present moment, Arsène Lupin is prowling around the station at Darnétal. At ten fifty, that is, in twenty-two minutes from now, he will take the train that goes from Rouen to Amiens."

"Do you think so? How do you know it?"

"Oh! It is quite simple. While we were in the car, Arsène Lupin consulted my railway guide. Why did he do it? Was there, not far from the spot where he disappeared, another line of railway, a station upon that line, and a train stopping at that station? On consulting my railway guide, I found such to be the case."

"Really, monsieur," said the commissary, "that is a marvellous deduction. I congratulate you on your skill."

I was now convinced that I had made a mistake in displaying so much cleverness. The commissary regarded me with astonishment, and I thought a slight suspicion entered his official mind ... Oh! Scarcely that, for the photographs distributed broadcast by the police department were too imperfect; they presented an Arsène Lupin so different from the one he had before him, that he could not possibly recognize me by it. But, all the same, he was troubled, confused and ill-at-ease.

"Mon Dieu! Nothing stimulates the comprehension so much as the loss of a pocketbook and the desire to recover it. And it seems to me that if you will give me two of your men, we may be able ..."

"Oh! I beg of you, monsieur le commissaire," cried Madame Renaud, "listen to Monsieur Berlat."

The intervention of my excellent friend was decisive.

Pronounced by her, the wife of an influential official, the name of Berlat became really my own, and gave me an identity that no mere suspicion could affect. The commissary arose, and said:

"Believe me, Monsieur Berlat, I shall be delighted to see you succeed. I am as much interested as you are in the arrest of Arsène Lupin."

He accompanied me to the automobile, and introduced two of his men, Honouré Massol and Gaston Delivet, who were assigned to assist me. My chauffeur cranked up the car and I took my place at the wheel. A few seconds later, we left the station. I was saved.

Ah! I must confess that in rolling over the boulevards that surrounded the old Norman city, in my swift thirty-five horse-power Moreau-Lepton, I experienced a deep feeling of pride, and the motor responded, sympathetically to my desires. At right and left, the trees flew past us with startling rapidity, and I, free, out of danger, had simply to arrange my little personal affairs with the two honest representatives of the Rouen police who were sitting behind me. Arsène Lupin was going in search of Arsène Lupin!

Modest guardians of social order – Gaston Delivet and Honouré Massol – how valuable was your assistance! What would I have done without you? Without you, many times, at the crossroads, I might have taken the wrong route! Without you, Arsène Lupin would have made a mistake, and the other would have escaped!

But the end was not yet. Far from it. I had yet to capture the thief and recover the stolen papers. Under no circumstances must my two acolytes be permitted to see those papers, much less to seize them. That was a point that might give me some difficulty.

We arrived at Darnétal three minutes after the departure of the train. True, I had the consolation of learning that a man wearing a grey overcoat with a black velvet collar had taken the train at the station. He had bought a second-class ticket for Amiens. Certainly, my début as detective was a promising one.

Delivet said to me:

"The train is express, and the next stop is Montérolier-Buchy in nineteen minutes. If we do not reach there before Arsène Lupin, he can proceed to Amiens, or change for the train going to Clères, and, from that point, reach Dieppe or Paris."

"How far to Montérolier?"

"Twenty-three kilometres."

"Twenty-three kilometres in nineteen minutes ... We will be there ahead of him."

We were off again! Never had my faithful Moreau-Repton responded to my impatience with such ardour and regularity. It participated in my anxiety. It endorsed my determination. It comprehended my animosity against that rascally Arsène Lupin. The knave! The traitor!

"Turn to the right," cried Delivet, "then to the left."

We fairly flew, scarcely touching the ground. The milestones looked like little timid beasts that vanished at our approach. Suddenly, at a turn of the road, we saw a vortex of smoke. It was the Northern Express. For a kilometre, it was a struggle, side by side, but an unequal struggle in which the issue was certain. We won the race by twenty lengths.

In three seconds we were on the platform standing before the second-class carriages. The doors were opened, and some passengers alighted, but not my thief. We made a search through the compartments. No sign of Arsène Lupin.

"Sapristi!" I cried, "he must have recognized me in the automobile as we were racing, side by side, and he leaped from the train."

"Ah! There he is now! crossing the track."

I started in pursuit of the man, followed by my two acolytes, or rather followed by one of them, for the other, Massol, proved himself to be a runner of exceptional speed and endurance. In a few moments, he had made an appreciable gain upon the fugitive. The man noticed it, leaped over a hedge, scampered across a meadow, and entered a thick grove. When we reached this grove, Massol was waiting for us. He went no farther, for fear of losing us.

"Quite right, my dear friend," I said. "After such a run, our victim must be out of wind. We will catch him now."

I examined the surroundings with the idea of proceeding alone in the arrest of the fugitive, in order to recover my papers, concerning which the authorities would doubtless ask many disagreeable questions. Then I returned to my companions, and said:

"It is all quite easy. You, Massol, take your place at the left; you, Delivet, at the right. From there, you can observe the entire posterior line of the bush, and he cannot escape without you seeing him, except by that ravine, and I shall watch it. If he does not come out voluntarily, I will enter and drive him out toward one or the other of you.

You have simply to wait. Ah! I forgot: in case I need you, a pistol shot."

Massol and Delivet walked away to their respective posts. As soon as they had disappeared, I entered the grove with the greatest precaution so as to be neither seen nor heard. I encountered dense thickets, through which narrow paths had been cut, but the overhanging boughs compelled me to adopt a stooping posture. One of these paths led to a clearing in which I found footsteps upon the wet grass. I followed them; they led me to the foot of a mound which was surmounted by a deserted, dilapidated hovel.

"He must be there," I said to myself. "It is a well-chosen retreat."

I crept cautiously to the side of the building. A slight noise informed me that he was there; and, then, through an opening, I saw him. His back was turned toward me. In two bounds, I was upon him. He tried to fire a revolver that he held in his hand. But he had no time. I threw him to the ground, in such a manner that his arms were beneath him, twisted and helpless, whilst I held him down with my knee on his breast.

"Listen, my boy," I whispered in his ear. "I am Arsène Lupin. You are to deliver over to me, immediately and gracefully, my pocketbook and the lady's jewels, and, in return therefore, I will save you from the police and enrol you amongst my friends. One word: yes or no?"

"Yes," he murmured.

"Very good. Your escape, this morning, was well planned. I congratulate you."

I arose. He fumbled in his pocket, drew out a large knife and tried to strike me with it.

"Imbecile!" I exclaimed.

With one hand, I parried the attack; with the other, I gave him a sharp blow on the carotid artery. He fell – stunned!

In my pocketbook, I recovered my papers and banknotes. Out of curiosity, I took his. Upon an envelope, addressed to him, I read his name: Pierre Onfrey. It startled me. Pierre Onfrey, the assassin of the rue Lafontaine at Auteuil! Pierre Onfrey, he who had cut the throats of Madame Delbois and her two daughters. I leaned over him. Yes, those were the features which, in the compartment, had evoked in me the memory of a face I could not then recall.

But time was passing. I placed in an envelope two bank-notes of one hundred francs each, with a card bearing these words: 'Arsène Lupin to his worthy colleagues Honouré Massol and Gaston Delivet, as a slight token of his gratitude.' I placed it in a prominent spot in the room, where they would be sure to find it. Beside it, I placed Madame Renaud's handbag. Why could I not return it to the lady who had befriended me? I must confess that I had taken from it everything that possessed any interest or value, leaving there only a shell comb, a stick of rouge Dorin for the lips, and an empty purse. But, you know, business is business. And then, really, her husband is engaged in such a dishonourable vocation!

The man was becoming conscious. What was I to do? I was unable to save him or condemn him. So I took his revolver and fired a shot in the air.

"My two acolytes will come and attend to his case," I said to myself, as I hastened away by the road through the ravine. Twenty minutes later, I was seated in my automobile.

At four o'clock, I telegraphed to my friends at Rouen that an unexpected event would prevent me from making my promised visit. Between ourselves, considering what my friends must now know, my visit is postponed indefinitely. A cruel disillusion for them!

At six o'clock I was in Paris. The evening newspapers informed me that Pierre Onfrey had been captured at last.

Next day, – let us not despise the advantages of judicious advertising, – the *Echo de France* published this sensational item:

Yesterday, near Buchy, after numerous exciting incidents, Arsène Lupin effected the arrest of Pierre Onfrey. The assassin of the rue Lafontaine had robbed Madame Renaud, wife of the director in the penitentiary service, in a railway carriage on the Paris-Havre line. Arsène Lupin restored to Madame Renaud the handbag that contained her jewels, and gave a generous recompense to the two detectives who had assisted him in making that dramatic arrest.

THE QUEEN'S
NECKLACE

Two or three times each year, on occasions of unusual importance, such as the balls at the Austrian Embassy or the soirées of Lady Billingstone, the Countess de Dreux-Soubise wore upon her white shoulders 'The Queen's Necklace'.

It was, indeed, the famous necklace, the legendary necklace that Bohmer and Bassenge, court jewellers, had made for Madame Du Barry; the veritable necklace that the Cardinal de Rohan-Soubise intended to give to Marie Antoinette, Queen of France; and the same that the adventuress Jeanne de Valois, Countess de la Motte, had pulled to pieces one evening in February, 1785, with the aid of her husband and their accomplice, Rétaux de Villette.

To tell the truth, the mounting alone was genuine. Rétaux de Villette had kept it, whilst the Count de la Motte and his wife scattered to the four winds of heaven the beautiful stones so carefully chosen by Bohmer. Later, he sold the mounting to Gaston de Dreux-Soubise, nephew and heir of the Cardinal, who repurchased the few diamonds that remained in the possession of the English jeweller, Jeffreys; supplemented them with other stones of the same size but of much inferior quality, and thus restored the marvellous necklace to the form in which it had come from the hands of Bohmer and Bassenge.

For nearly a century, the house of Dreux-Soubise had prided itself upon the possession of this historic jewel. Although adverse circumstances had greatly reduced their fortune, they preferred to curtail their household expenses rather than part with this relic of royalty. More particularly, the present count clung to it as a man clings to the home of his ancestors. As a matter of prudence, he had rented a safety-deposit box at the Crédit Lyonnais in which to keep it. He went for it himself on the afternoon of the day on which his wife wished to wear it, and he, himself, carried it back next morning.

On this particular evening, at the reception given at the Palais de Castille, the Countess achieved a remarkable success; and King Christian, in whose honour the fête was given, commented on her grace and beauty. The thousand facets of the diamond sparkled and shone like flames of fire about her shapely neck and shoulders, and it is safe to say that none but she could have borne the weight of such an ornament with so much ease and grace.

This was a double triumph, and the Count de Dreux was highly elated when they returned to their chamber in the old house of the faubourg Saint-Germain. He was proud of his wife, and quite as proud, perhaps, of the necklace that had conferred added lustre to his noble house for generations. His wife, also, regarded the necklace with an almost childish vanity, and it was not without regret that she removed it from her shoulders and handed it to her husband who admired it as passionately as if he had never seen it before. Then, having placed it in its case of red leather, stamped with the Cardinal's arms, he passed into an adjoining room which was simply an alcove or cabinet that had been cut off from their chamber, and which could be entered only by means of a door at the foot of their bed. As he had done on previous occasions, he hid it on a high shelf amongst hat boxes and piles of linen. He closed the door, and retired.

Next morning, he arose about nine o'clock, intending to go to the Crédit Lyonnais before breakfast. He dressed, drank a cup of coffee, and went to the stables to give his orders. The condition of one of the horses worried him. He caused it to be exercised in his presence. Then he returned to his wife, who had not yet left the chamber. Her maid was dressing her hair. When her husband entered, she asked:

"Are you going out?"

"Yes, as far as the bank."

"Of course. That is wise."

He entered the cabinet; but, after a few seconds, and without any sign of astonishment, he asked:

"Did you take it, my dear?"

"What? No, I have not taken anything."

"You must have moved it."

"Not at all. I have not even opened that door."

He appeared at the door, disconcerted, and stammered, in a scarcely intelligible voice:

"You haven't ... It wasn't you? Then ..."

She hastened to his assistance and together they made a thorough search, throwing the boxes to the floor and overturning the piles of linen. Then the count said, quite discouraged:

"It is useless to look any more. I put it here, on this shelf."

"You must be mistaken."

"No, no, it was on this shelf – nowhere else."

They lighted a candle, as the room was quite dark, and then carried out all the linen and other articles that the room contained. And, when the room was emptied, they confessed, in despair, that the famous necklace had disappeared. Without losing time in vain lamentations, the countess notified the commissary of police, Monsiuer Valorbe, who came at once, and, after hearing their story, inquired of the count:

"Are you sure that no one passed through your chamber during the night?"

"Absolutely sure, as I am a very light sleeper. Besides, the chamber door was bolted, and I remember unbolting it this morning when my wife rang for her maid."

"And there is no other entrance to the cabinet?"

"None."

"No windows?"

"Yes, but it is closed up."

"I will look at it."

Candles were lighted, and Monsieur Valorbe observed at once that the lower half of the window was covered by a large press which was, however, so narrow that it did not touch the casement on either side.

"On what does this window open?"

"A small inner court."

"And you have a floor above this?"

"Two; but, on a level with the servant's floor, there is a close grating over the court. That is why this room is so dark."

When the press was moved, they found that the window was fastened, which would not have been the case if anyone had entered that way.

"Unless," said the count, "they went out through our chamber."

"In that case, you would have found the door unbolted."

The commissary considered the situation for a moment, then asked the countess:

"Did any of your servants know that you wore the necklace last evening?"

"Certainly; I didn't conceal the fact. But nobody knew that it was hidden in that cabinet."

"No one?"

"No one ... unless ..."

"Be quite sure, madam, as it is a very important point."

She turned to her husband, and said:

"I was thinking of Henriette."

"Henriette? She didn't know where we kept it."

"Are you sure?"

"Who is this woman Henriette?" asked Monsieur Valorbe.

"A schoolmate, who was disowned by her family for marrying beneath her. After her husband's death,

I furnished an apartment in this house for her and her son. She is clever with her needle and has done some work for me."

"What floor is she on?"

"Same as ours ... at the end of the corridor ... and I think ... the window of her kitchen ..."

"Opens on this little court, does it not?"

"Yes, just opposite ours."

Monsieur Valorbe then asked to see Henriette. They went to her apartment; she was sewing, whilst her son Raoul, about six years old, was sitting beside her, reading. The commissary was surprised to see the wretched apartment that had been provided for the woman. It consisted of one room without a fireplace, and a very small room that served as a kitchen. The commissary proceeded to question her. She appeared to be overwhelmed on learning of the theft. Last evening she had herself dressed the countess and placed the necklace upon her shoulders.

"Good God!" she exclaimed, "it can't be possible!"

"And you have no idea? Not the least suspicion? Is it possible that the thief may have passed through your room?"

She laughed heartily, never supposing that she could be an object of suspicion.

"But I have not left my room. I never go out. And, perhaps, you have not seen?"

She opened the kitchen window, and said:

"See, it is at least three metres to the ledge of the opposite window."

"Who told you that we supposed the theft might have been committed in that way?"

"But ... the necklace was in the cabinet, wasn't it?"

"How do you know that?"

"Why, I have always known that it was kept there at night. It had been mentioned in my presence."

Her face, though still young, bore unmistakable traces of sorrow and resignation. And it now assumed an expression of anxiety as if some danger threatened her. She drew her son toward her. The child took her hand, and kissed it affectionately.

When they were alone again, the count said to the commissary:

"I do not suppose you suspect Henriette. I can answer for her. She is honesty itself."

"I quite agree with you," replied Monsieur Valorbe. "At most, I thought there might have been an unconscious complicity. But I confess that even that theory must be abandoned, as it does not help solve the problem now before us."

The commissary of police abandoned the investigation, which was now taken up and completed by the examining judge. He questioned the servants, examined the condition of the bolt, experimented with the opening and closing of the cabinet window, and explored the little court from top to bottom. All was in vain. The bolt was intact. The window could not be opened or closed from the outside.

The inquiries especially concerned Henriette, for, in spite of everything, they always turned in her direction. They made a thorough investigation of her past life, and ascertained that, during the last three years, she had left the house only four times, and her business on those occasions was satisfactorily explained. As a matter of fact, she acted as chambermaid and seamstress to the countess, who treated her with great strictness and even severity.

At the end of a week, the examining judge had secured no more definite information than the commissary of police. The judge said:

"Admitting that we know the guilty party, which we do not, we are confronted by the fact that we do not know how the theft was committed. We are brought face to face with two obstacles: a door and a window – both closed and fastened. It is thus a double mystery. How could anyone enter, and, moreover, how could anyone escape, leaving behind him a bolted door and a fastened window?"

At the end of four months, the secret opinion of the judge was that the count and countess, being hard pressed for money, which was their normal condition, had sold the Queen's Necklace. He closed the investigation.

The loss of the famous jewel was a severe blow to the Dreux-Soubise. Their credit being no longer propped up by the reserve fund that such a treasure constituted, they found themselves confronted by more exacting creditors and money-lenders. They were obliged to cut down to the quick, to sell or mortgage every article that possessed any commercial value. In brief, it would have been their ruin, if two large legacies from some distant relatives had not saved them.

Their pride also suffered a downfall, as if they had lost a quartering from their escutcheon. And, strange to relate, it was upon her former schoolmate, Henriette, that the countess vented her spleen. Toward her, the countess displayed the most spiteful feelings, and even openly accused her. First, Henriette was relegated to the servants' quarters, and, next day, discharged.

For some time, the count and countess passed an uneventful life. They traveled a great deal. Only one incident of record occurred during that period. Some months after the departure of Henriette, the countess was surprised when she received and read the following letter, signed by Henriette:

> *Madame,*
>
> *I do not know how to thank you; for it was you, was it not, who sent me that? It could not have been anyone else. No one but you knows where I live. If I am wrong, excuse me, and accept my sincere thanks for your past favours ...*

What did the letter mean? The present or past favours of the countess consisted principally of injustice and neglect. Why, then, this letter of thanks?

When asked for an explanation, Henriette replied that she had received a letter, through the mails, enclosing two banknotes of one thousand francs each. The envelope, which she enclosed with her reply, bore the Paris postmark, and was addressed in a handwriting that was obviously disguised. Now, whence came those two thousand francs? Who had sent them? And why had they sent them?

Henriette received a similar letter and a like sum of money twelve months later. And a third time; and a fourth; and each year for a period of six years, with this difference, that in the fifth and sixth years the sum was doubled. There was another difference: the post-office authorities having seized one of the letters under the pretext that it was not registered, the last two letters were duly sent according to the postal regulations, the first dated from Saint-Germain, the other from Suresnes. The writer signed the first one, 'Anquety'; and the other, 'Péchard.' The addresses that he gave were false.

At the end of six years, Henriette died, and the mystery remained unsolved.

* * *

All these events are known to the public. The case was one of those which excite public interest, and it was a strange coincidence that this necklace, which had caused such a great commotion in France at the close of the eighteenth century, should create a similar commotion a century later. But what I am about to relate is known only to the parties directly interested and a few others from whom the count exacted a promise of secrecy. As it is probable that someday or other that promise will be broken, I have no hesitation in rending the veil and thus disclosing the key to the mystery, the explanation of the letter published in the morning papers two days ago; an extraordinary letter which increased, if possible, the mists and shadows that envelope this inscrutable drama.

Five days ago, a number of guests were dining with the Count de Dreux-Soubise. There were several ladies present, including his two nieces and his cousin, and the following gentlemen: the President of Essaville, the

Deputy Bochas, the Chevalier Floriani, whom the count had known in Sicily, and General Marquis de Rouzières, an old club friend.

After the repast, coffee was served by the ladies, who gave the gentlemen permission to smoke their cigarettes, provided they would not desert the salon. The conversation was general, and finally one of the guests chanced to speak of celebrated crimes. And that gave the Marquis de Rouzières, who delighted to tease the count, an opportunity to mention the affair of the Queen's Necklace, a subject that the count detested.

Each one expressed his own opinion of the affair; and, of course, their various theories were not only contradictory but impossible.

"And you, monsieur," said the countess to the Chevalier Floriani, "what is your opinion?"

"Oh! I – I have no opinion, madame."

All the guests protested; for the chevalier had just related in an entertaining manner various adventures in which he had participated with his father, a magistrate at Palermo, and which established his judgment and taste in such manners.

"I confess," said he, "I have sometimes succeeded in unravelling mysteries that the cleverest detectives have renounced; yet I do not claim to be Herlock Sholmes. Moreover, I know very little about the affair of the Queen's Necklace."

Everybody now turned to the count, who was thus obliged, quite unwillingly, to narrate all the circumstances connected with the theft. The chevalier listened, reflected, asked a few questions, and said:

"It is very strange ... at first sight, the problem appears to be a very simple one."

The count shrugged his shoulders. The others drew closer to the chevalier, who continued, in a dogmatic tone:

"As a general rule, in order to find the author of a crime or a theft, it is necessary to determine how that crime or theft was committed, or, at least, how it could have been committed. In the present case, nothing is more simple, because we are face to face, not with several theories, but with one positive fact, that is to say: the thief could only enter by the chamber door or the window of the cabinet. Now, a person cannot open a bolted door from the outside. Therefore, he must have entered through the window."

"But it was closed and fastened, and we found it fastened afterward," declared the count.

"In order to do that," continued Floriani, without heeding the interruption, "he had simply to construct a bridge, a plank or a ladder, between the balcony of the kitchen and the ledge of the window, and as the jewel case—"

"But I repeat that the window was fastened," exclaimed the count, impatiently.

This time, Floriani was obliged to reply. He did so with the greatest tranquillity, as if the objection was the most insignificant affair in the world.

"I will admit that it was; but is there not a transom in the upper part of the window?"

"How do you know that?"

"In the first place, that was customary in houses of that

date; and, in the second place, without such a transom, the theft cannot be explained."

"Yes, there is one, but it was closed, the same as the window. Consequently, we did not pay attention to it."

"That was a mistake; for, if you had examined it, you would have found that it had been opened."

"But how?"

"I presume that, like all others, it opens by means of a wire with a ring on the lower end."

"Yes, but I do not see–"

"Now, through a hole in the window, a person could, by the aid of some instrument, let us say a poker with a hook at the end, grip the ring, pull down, and open the transom."

The count laughed and said:

"Excellent! excellent! Your scheme is very cleverly constructed, but you overlook one thing, monsieur, there is no hole in the window."

"There was a hole."

"Nonsense, we would have seen it."

"In order to see it, you must look for it, and no one has looked. The hole is there; it must be there, at the side of the window, in the putty. In a vertical direction, of course."

The count arose. He was greatly excited. He paced up and down the room, two or three times, in a nervous manner; then, approaching Floriani, said:

"Nobody has been in that room since; nothing has been changed."

"Very well, monsieur, you can easily satisfy yourself that my explanation is correct."

"It does not agree with the facts established by the

examining judge. You have seen nothing, and yet you contradict all that we have seen and all that we know."

Floriani paid no attention to the count's petulance. He simply smiled and said:

"Mon Dieu, monsieur, I submit my theory; that is all. If I am mistaken, you can easily prove it."

"I will do so at once ... I confess that your assurance–"

The count muttered a few more words; then suddenly rushed to the door and left the room. Not a word was uttered in his absence; and this profound silence gave the situation an air of almost tragic importance. Finally, the count returned. He was pale and nervous. He said to his friends, in a trembling voice:

"I beg your pardon ... the revelations of the chevalier were so unexpected ... I should never have thought ..."

His wife questioned him, eagerly:

"Speak ... what is it?"

He stammered: "The hole is there, at the very spot, at the side of the window–"

He seized the chevalier's arm, and said to him in an imperious tone:

"Now, monsieur, proceed. I admit that you are right so far, but now ... that is not all ... go on ... tell us the rest of it."

Floriani disengaged his arm gently, and, after a moment, continued:

"Well, in my opinion, this is what happened. The thief, knowing that the countess was going to wear the necklace that evening, had prepared his gangway or bridge during your absence. He watched you through the window and saw you hide the necklace. Afterward, he cut the glass and pulled the ring."

"Ah! but the distance was so great that it would be impossible for him to reach the window fastening through the transom."

"Well, then, if he could not open the window by reaching through the transom, he must have crawled through the transom."

"Impossible; it is too small. No man could crawl through it."

"Then it was not a man," declared Floriani.

"What!"

"If the transom is too small to admit a man, it must have been a child."

"A child!"

"Did you not say that your friend Henriette had a son?"

"Yes; a son named Raoul."

"Then, in all probability, it was Raoul who committed the theft."

"What proof have you of that?"

"What proof! Plenty of it ... For instance—"

He stopped, and reflected for a moment, then continued:

"For instance, that gangway or bridge. It is improbable that the child could have brought it in from outside the house and carried it away again without being observed. He must have used something close at hand. In the little room used by Henriette as a kitchen, were there not some shelves against the wall on which she placed her pans and dishes?"

"Two shelves, to the best of my memory."

"Are you sure that those shelves are really fastened to the wooden brackets that support them? For, if they are not, we could be justified in presuming that the child removed them, fastened them together, and thus formed his bridge. Perhaps, also, since there was a stove, we might find the bent poker that he used to open the transom."

Without saying a word, the count left the room; and, this time, those present did not feel the nervous anxiety they had experienced the first time. They were confident that Floriani was right, and no one was surprised when the count returned and declared:

"It was the child. Everything proves it."

"You have seen the shelves and the poker?"

"Yes. The shelves have been unnailed, and the poker is there yet."

But the countess exclaimed:

"You had better say it was his mother. Henriette is the guilty party. She must have compelled her son–"

"No," declared the chevalier, "the mother had nothing to do with it."

"Nonsense! They occupied the same room. The child could not have done it without the mother's knowledge."

"True, they lived in the same room, but all this happened in the adjoining room, during the night, while the mother was asleep."

"And the necklace?" said the count. "It would have been found amongst the child's things."

"Pardon me! He had been out. That morning, on which you found him reading, he had just come from school, and perhaps the commissary of police, instead of wasting his time on the innocent mother, would have been better employed in searching the child's desk amongst his school books."

"But how do you explain those two thousand francs that Henriette received each year? Are they not evidence of her complicity?"

"If she had been an accomplice, would she have thanked you for that money? And then, was she not closely watched? But the child, being free, could easily go to a neighbouring city, negotiate with some dealer and sell him one diamond or two diamonds, as he might wish, upon condition that the money should be sent from Paris, and that proceeding could be repeated from year to year."

An indescribable anxiety oppressed the Dreux-Soubise and their guests. There was something in the tone and attitude of Floriani – something more than the chevalier's assurance which, from the beginning, had so annoyed the count. There was a touch of irony, that seemed rather hostile than sympathetic. But the count affected to laugh, as he said:

"All that is very ingenious and interesting, and I congratulate you upon your vivid imagination."

"No, not at all," replied Floriani, with the utmost gravity, "I imagine nothing. I simply describe the events as they must have occurred."

"But what do you know about them?"

"What you yourself have told me. I picture to myself the life of the mother and child down there in the country; the illness of the mother, the schemes of and inventions of the child to sell the precious stones in order to save his mother's life, or, at least, soothe her dying moments. Her illness overcomes her. She dies. Years roll on. The child becomes a man; and then – and now I will give my imagination a free rein – let us suppose that the man feels a desire to return to the home of his childhood, that he does so, and that he meets there certain people who suspect and accuse his mother ... do you realize the sorrow and anguish of such an interview in the very house wherein the original drama was played?"

His words seemed to echo for a few seconds in the ensuing silence, and one could read upon the faces of the Count and Countess de Dreux a bewildered effort to comprehend his meaning and, at the same time, the fear and anguish of such a comprehension. The count spoke at last, and said:

"Who are you, monsieur?"

"I? The Chevalier Floriani, whom you met at Palermo, and whom you have been gracious enough to invite to your house on several occasions."

"Then what does this story mean?"

"Oh! Nothing at all! It is simply a pastime, so far as I am concerned. I endeavour to depict the pleasure that Henriette's son, if he still lives, would have in telling you that he was the guilty party, and that he did it because his mother was unhappy, as she was on the point of losing the place of a ... servant, by which she lived, and because the child suffered at sight of his mother's sorrow."

He spoke with suppressed emotion, rose partially and inclined toward the countess. There could be no doubt that the Chevalier Floriani was Henriette's son. His attitude and words proclaimed it. Besides, was it not his obvious intention and desire to be recognized as such?

The count hesitated. What action would he take against the audacious guest? Ring? Provoke a scandal? Unmask the man who had once robbed him? But that was a long time ago! And who would believe that absurd story about the guilty child? No; better far to accept the situation, and pretend not to comprehend the true meaning of it. So the count, turning to Floriani, exclaimed:

"Your story is very curious, very entertaining; I enjoyed it much. But what do you think has become of this young man, this model son? I hope he has not abandoned the career in which he made such a brilliant début."

"Oh! Certainly not."

"After such a début! To steal the Queen's Necklace at six years of age; the celebrated necklace that was coveted by Marie-Antoinette!"

"And to steal it," remarked Floriani, falling in with the count's mood, "without costing him the slightest trouble, without anyone thinking to examine the condition of the window, or to observe that the window-sill was too clean – that windowsill which he had wiped in order to efface the marks he had made in the thick dust. We must admit that it was sufficient to turn the head of a boy at that age. It was all so easy. He had simply to desire the thing, and reach out his hand to get it."

"And he reached out his hand."

"Both hands," replied the chevalier, laughing.

His companions received a shock. What mystery surrounded the life of the so-called Floriani? How wonderful must have been the life of that adventurer, a thief at six years of age, and who, today, in search of excitement or, at most, to gratify a feeling of resentment, had come to brave his victim in her own house, audaciously, foolishly, and yet with all the grace and delicacy of a courteous guest!

He arose and approached the countess to bid her adieu. She recoiled, unconsciously. He smiled.

"Oh! Madame, you are afraid of me! Did I pursue my role of parlour magician a step too far?"

She controlled herself, and replied, with her accustomed ease:

"Not at all, monsieur. The legend of that dutiful son interested me very much, and I am pleased to know that my necklace had such a brilliant destiny. But do you not think that the son of that woman, that Henriette, was the victim of hereditary influence in the choice of his vocation?"

He shuddered, feeling the point, and replied:

"I am sure of it; and, moreover, his natural tendency to crime must have been very strong or he would have been discouraged."

"Why so?"

"Because, as you must know, the majority of the diamonds were false. The only genuine stones were the few purchased from the English jeweller, the others having been sold, one by one, to meet the cruel necessities of life."

"It was still the Queen's Necklace, monsieur," replied the countess, haughtily, "and that is something that he, Henriette's son, could not appreciate."

"He was able to appreciate, madame, that, whether true or false, the necklace was nothing more that an object of parade, an emblem of senseless pride."

The count made a threatening gesture, but his wife stopped him.

"Monsieur," she said, "if the man to whom you allude has the slightest sense of honour–"

She stopped, intimidated by Floriani's cool manner.

"If that man has the slightest sense of honour," he repeated.

She felt that she would not gain anything by speaking to him in that manner, and in spite of her anger and indignation, trembling as she was from humiliated pride, she said to him, almost politely:

"Monsieur, the legend says that Rétaux de Villette, when in possession of the Queen's Necklace, did not disfigure the mounting. He understood that the diamonds were simply the ornament, the accessory, and that the mounting was the essential work, the creation of the artist, and he respected it accordingly. Do you think that this man had the same feeling?"

"I have no doubt that the mounting still exists. The child respected it."

"Well, monsieur, if you should happen to meet him, will you tell him that he unjustly keeps possession of a relic that is the property and pride of a certain family, and that, although the stones have been removed, the Queen's necklace still belongs to the house of Dreux-Soubise. It belongs to us as much as our name or our honour."

The chevalier replied, simply:

"I shall tell him, madame."

He bowed to her, saluted the count and the other guests, and departed.

* * *

Four days later, the countess de Dreux found upon the table in her chamber a red leather case bearing the cardinal's arms. She opened it, and found the Queen's Necklace.

But as all things must, in the life of a man who strives for unity and logic, converge toward the same goal—and as a little advertising never does any harm – on the following day, the *Echo de France* published these sensational lines:

The Queen's Necklace, the famous historical jewellery stolen from the family of Dreux-Soubise, has been recovered by Arsène Lupin, who hastened to restore it to its rightful owner. We cannot too highly commend such a delicate and chivalrous act.

THE SEVEN
OF HEARTS

I am frequently asked this question: "How did you make the acquaintance of Arsène Lupin?"

My connection with Arsène Lupin was well known. The details that I gather concerning that mysterious man, the irrefutable facts that I present, the new evidence that I produce, the interpretation that I place on certain acts of which the public has seen only the exterior manifestations without being able to discover the secret reasons or the invisible mechanism, all establish, if not an intimacy, at least amicable relations and regular confidences.

But how did I make his acquaintance? Why was I selected to be his historiographer? Why I, and not someone else?

The answer is simple: chance alone presided over my choice; my merit was not considered. It was chance that put me in his way. It was by chance that I was participant in one of his strangest and most mysterious adventures; and by chance that I was an actor in a drama of which he was the marvellous stage director; an obscure and intricate drama, bristling with such thrilling events that I feel a certain embarrassment in undertaking to describe it.

The first act takes place during that memorable night of the twenty-second of June, of which so much has already been said. And, for my part, I attribute the anomalous conduct of which I was guilty on that occasion to the unusual frame of mind in which I found myself on my return home. I had dined with some friends at the Cascade restaurant, and, the entire evening, whilst we smoked and the orchestra played melancholy waltzes, we talked only of crimes and thefts, and dark and frightful intrigues. That is always a poor overture to a night's sleep.

The Saint-Martins went away in an automobile. Jean Daspry – that delightful, heedless Daspry who, six months later, was killed in such a tragic manner on the frontier of Morocco – Jean Daspry and I returned on foot through the dark, warm night. When we arrived in front of the little house in which I had lived for a year at Neuilly, on the boulevard Maillot, he said to me:

"Are you afraid?"

"What an idea!"

"But this house is so isolated ... no neighbours ... vacant lots ... Really, I am not a coward, and yet–"

"Well, you are very cheering, I must say."

"Oh! I say that as I would say anything else. The Saint-Martins have impressed me with their stories of brigands and thieves."

We shook hands and said goodnight. I took out my key and opened the door.

"Well, that is good," I murmured, "Antoine has forgotten to light a candle."

Then I recalled the fact that Antoine was away; I had given him a short leave of absence. Forthwith, I was disagreeably oppressed by the darkness and silence of the night. I ascended the stairs on tiptoe, and reached my room as quickly as possible; then, contrary to my usual habit, I turned the key and pushed the bolt.

The light of my candle restored my courage. Yet I was careful to take my revolver from its case – a large, powerful weapon – and place it beside my bed. That precaution completed my reassurance. I laid down and, as usual, took a book from my night table to read myself to sleep. Then I received a great surprise. Instead of the paperknife with which I had marked my place on the preceding, I found an envelope, closed with five seals of red wax. I seized it eagerly. It was addressed to me, and marked: 'Urgent.'

A letter! A letter addressed to me! Who could have put it in that place? Nervously, I tore open the envelope, and read:

From the moment you open this letter, whatever happens, whatever you may hear, do not move, do not utter one cry. Otherwise you are doomed.

I am not a coward, and, quite as well as another, I can face real danger, or smile at the visionary perils of imagination. But, let me repeat, I was in an anomalous condition of mind, with my nerves set on edge by the events of the evening. Besides, was there not, in my present situation, something startling and mysterious, calculated to disturb the most courageous spirit?

My feverish fingers clutched the sheet of paper, and I read and reread those threatening words: 'Do not move, do not utter one cry. Otherwise, you are doomed.'

"Nonsense!" I thought. "It is a joke; the work of some cheerful idiot."

I was about to laugh – a good loud laugh. Who prevented me? What haunting fear compressed my throat?

At least, I would blow out the candle. No, I could not do it. 'Do not move, or you are doomed,' were the words he had written.

These auto-suggestions are frequently more imperious than the most positive realities; but why should I struggle against them? I had simply to close my eyes. I did so.

At that moment, I heard a slight noise, followed by crackling sounds, proceeding from a large room used by me as a library. A small room or antechamber was situated between the library and my bedchamber.

The approach of an actual danger greatly excited me, and I felt a desire to get up, seize my revolver, and rush into the library. I did not rise; I saw one of the curtains of the left window move. There was no doubt about it: the curtain had moved. It was still moving. And I saw – oh! I saw quite distinctly – in the narrow space between the curtains and the window, a human form; a bulky mass that prevented the curtains from hanging straight. And it is equally certain that the man saw me through the large meshes of the curtain. Then, I understood the situation. His mission was to guard me while the others carried away their booty. Should I rise and seize my revolver? Impossible! He was there! At the least movement, at the least cry, I was doomed.

Then came a terrific noise that shook the house; this was followed by lighter sounds, two or three together, like those of a hammer that rebounded. At least, that was the impression formed in my confused brain. These were mingled with other sounds, thus creating a veritable uproar which proved that the intruders were not only bold, but felt themselves secure from interruption.

They were right. I did not move. Was it cowardice? No, rather weakness, a total inability to move any portion of my body, combined with discretion; for why should I struggle? Behind that man, there were ten others who would come to his assistance. Should I risk my life to save a few tapestries and bibelots?

Throughout the night, my torture endured. Insufferable torture, terrible anguish! The noises had stopped, but I was in constant fear of their renewal. And the man! The man who was guarding me, weapon in hand. My fearful eyes remained cast in his direction. And my heart beat! And a profuse perspiration oozed from every pore of my body!

Suddenly, I experienced an immense relief; a milk-wagon, whose sound was familiar to me, passed along the boulevard; and, at the same time, I had an impression that the light of a new day was trying to steal through the closed window blinds.

At last, daylight penetrated the room; other vehicles passed along the boulevard; and all the phantoms of the night vanished. Then I put one arm out of the bed, slowly and cautiously. My eyes were fixed upon the curtain, locating the exact spot at which I must fire; I made an exact calculation of the movements I must make; then, quickly, I seized my revolver and fired.

I leaped from my bed with a cry of deliverance, and rushed to the window. The bullet had passed through the curtain and the window-glass, but it had not touched the man – for the very good reason that there was none there. Nobody! Thus, during the entire night, I had been hypnotized by a fold of the curtain. And, during that time, the malefactors ... Furiously, with an enthusiasm that nothing could have stopped, I turned the key, opened the door, crossed the antechamber, opened another door, and rushed into the library. But amazement stopped me on the threshold, panting, astounded, more astonished than I had been by the absence of the man. All the things that I supposed had been stolen, furniture, books, pictures, old tapestries, everything was in its proper place.

It was incredible. I could not believe my eyes. Notwithstanding that uproar, those noises of removal ... I made a tour, I inspected the walls, I made a mental inventory of all the familiar objects. Nothing was missing. And, what was more disconcerting, there was no clue to the intruders, not a sign, not a chair disturbed, not the trace of a footstep.

"Well! Well!" I said to myself, pressing my hands on my bewildered head, "surely I am not crazy! I heard something!"

Inch by inch, I made a careful examination of the room. It was in vain. Unless I could consider this as a discovery: Under a small Persian rug, I found a card – an ordinary playing card. It was the seven of hearts; it was like any other seven of hearts in French playing cards, with this slight but curious exception: The extreme point of each of the seven red spots or hearts was pierced by a hole, round and regular as if made with the point of an awl.

Nothing more. A card and a letter found in a book. But was not that sufficient to affirm that I had not been the plaything of a dream?

* * *

Throughout the day, I continued my searches in the library. It was a large room, much too large for the requirements of such a house, and the decoration of which attested the bizarre taste of its founder. The floor was a mosaic of multicoloured stones, formed into large symmetrical designs. The walls were covered with a similar mosaic, arranged in panels, Pompeiian allegories, Byzantine compositions, frescoes of the Middle Ages. A Bacchus bestriding a cask. An emperor wearing a gold crown, a flowing beard, and holding a sword in his right hand.

Quite high, after the style of an artist's studio, there was a large window – the only one in the room. That window being always open at night, it was probable that the men had entered through it, by the aid of a ladder. But, again, there was no evidence. The bottom of the ladder would have left some marks in the soft earth beneath the window; but there were none.

Nor were there any traces of footsteps in any part of the yard.

I had no idea of informing the police, because the facts I had before me were so absurd and inconsistent. They would laugh at me. However, as I was then a reporter on the staff of the *Gil Blas,* I wrote a lengthy account of my adventure and it was published in the paper on the second day thereafter. The article attracted some attention, but no one took it seriously. They regarded it as a work of fiction rather than a story of real life. The Saint-Martins rallied me. But Daspry, who took an interest in such matters, came to see me, made a study of the affair, but reached no conclusion.

A few mornings later, the doorbell rang, and Antoine came to inform me that a gentleman desired to see me. He would not give his name. I directed Antoine to show him up. He was a man of about forty years of age with a very dark complexion, lively features, and whose correct dress, slightly frayed, proclaimed a taste that contrasted strangely with his rather vulgar manners. Without any preamble, he said to me – in a rough voice that confirmed my suspicion as to his social position:

"Monsieur, whilst in a café, I picked up a copy of the *Gil Blas,* and read your article. It interested me very much.

"Thank you."

"And here I am."

"Ah!"

"Yes, to talk to you. Are all the facts related by you quite correct?"

"Absolutely so."

"Well, in that case, I can, perhaps, give you some information."

"Very well; proceed."

"No, not yet. First, I must be sure that the facts are exactly as you have related them."

"I have given you my word. What further proof do you want?"

"I must remain alone in this room."

"I do not understand," I said, with surprise.

"It's an idea that occurred to me when reading your article. Certain details established an extraordinary coincidence with another case that came under my notice. If I am mistaken, I shall say nothing more. And the only means of ascertaining the truth is by my remaining in the room alone."

What was at the bottom of this proposition? Later, I recalled that the man was exceedingly nervous; but, at the same time, although somewhat astonished, I found nothing particularly abnormal about the man or the request he had made. Moreover, my curiosity was aroused; so I replied:

"Very well. How much time do you require?"

"Oh! Three minutes – not longer. Three minutes from now, I will rejoin you."

I left the room, and went downstairs. I took out my watch. One minute passed. Two minutes. Why did I feel so depressed? Why did those moments seem so solemn and weird? Two minutes and a half ... Two minutes and three quarters. Then I heard a pistol shot.

I bounded up the stairs and entered the room. A cry of horror escaped me. In the middle of the room, the man was lying on his left side, motionless. Blood was flowing from a wound in his forehead. Near his hand was a revolver, still smoking.

But, in addition to this frightful spectacle, my attention was attracted by another object. At two feet from the body, upon the floor, I saw a playing card. It was the seven of hearts. I picked it up. The lower extremity of each of the seven spots was pierced with a small round hole.

* * *

A half-hour later, the commissary of police arrived, then the coroner and the chief of the Sûreté, Monsieur Dudouis. I had been careful not to touch the corpse. The preliminary inquiry was very brief, and disclosed nothing. There were no papers in the pockets of the deceased; no name upon his clothes; no initial upon his linen; nothing to give any clue to his identity. The room was in the same perfect order as before. The furniture had not been disturbed. Yet this man had not come to my house solely for the purpose of killing himself, or because he considered my place the most convenient one for his suicide! There must have been a motive for his act of despair, and that motive was, no doubt, the result of some new fact ascertained by him during the three minutes he was alone.

What was that fact? What had he seen? What frightful secret had been revealed to him? There was no answer to these questions. But, at the last moment, an incident occurred that appeared to us of considerable importance.

As two policemen were raising the body to place it on a stretcher, the left hand thus being disturbed, a crumpled card fell from it. The card bore these words: 'Georges Andermatt, 37 Rue de Berry.'

What did that mean? Georges Andermatt was a rich banker in Paris, the founder and president of the Metal Exchange which had given such an impulse to the metallic industries in France. He lived in princely style; was the possessor of numerous automobiles, coaches, and an expensive racing-stable. His social affairs were very select, and Madame Andermatt was noted for her grace and beauty.

"Can that be the man's name?" I asked.

The chief of the Sûreté leaned over him.

"It is not he. Monsieur Andermatt is a thin man, and slightly grey."

"But why this card?"

"Have you a telephone, monsieur?"

"Yes, in the vestibule. Come with me."

He looked in the directory, and then asked for number 415 21.

"Is Monsieur Andermatt at home? Please tell him that Monsieur Dudouis wished him to come at once to 102 Boulevard Maillot. Very important."

Twenty minutes later, Monsieur Andermatt arrived in his automobile. After the circumstances had been explained to him, he was taken in to see the corpse. He displayed considerable emotion, and spoke, in a low tone, and apparently unwillingly:

"Etienne Varin," he said.

"You know him?"

"No ... or, at least, yes ... by sight only. His brother ..."

"Ah! He has a brother?"

"Yes, Alfred Varin. He came to see me once on some matter of business ... I forget what it was."

"Where does he live?"

"The two brothers live together – rue de Provence, I think."

"Do you know any reason why he should commit suicide?"

"None."

"He held a card in his hand. It was your card with your address."

"I do not understand that. It must have been there by some coincidence that will be disclosed by the investigation."

A very strange coincidence, I thought; and I felt that the others entertained the same opinion.

I discovered the same opinion in the papers next day, and amongst all my friends with whom I discussed the affair. Amid the mysteries that enveloped it, after the double discovery of the seven of hearts pierced with seven holes, after the two inscrutable events that had happened in my house, that visiting card promised to throw some light on the affair. Through it, the truth may be revealed. But, contrary to our expectations, Monsieur Andermatt furnished no explanation. He said:

"I have told you all I know. What more can I do? I am greatly surprised that my card should be found in such a place, and I sincerely hope the point will be cleared up."

It was not. The official investigation established that the Varin brothers were of Swiss origin, had led a shifting life under various names, frequenting gambling resorts, associating with a band of foreigners who had been dispersed by the police after a series of robberies in which their participation was established only by their flight. At number 24 rue de Provence, where the Varin brothers had lived six years before, no one knew what had become of them.

I confess that, for my part, the case seemed to me so complicated and so mysterious that I did not think the problem would ever be solved, so I concluded to waste no more time upon it. But Jean Daspry, whom I frequently met at that period, became more and more interested in it each day. It was he who pointed out to me that item from a foreign newspaper which was reproduced and commented upon by the entire press. It read as follows:

The first trial of a new model of submarine boat, which is expected to revolutionize naval warfare, will be given in presence of the former Emperor at a place that will be kept secret until the last minute. An indiscretion has revealed its name; it is called 'The Seven-of-Hearts.'

The Seven-of-Hearts! That presented a new problem. Could a connection be established between the name of the submarine and the incidents which we have related? But a connection of what nature? What had happened here could have no possible relation with the submarine.

"What do you know about it?" said Daspry to me. "The most diverse effects often proceed from the same cause."

Two days later, the following foreign news item was received and published:

"It is said that the plans of the new submarine 'Seven-of-Hearts' were prepared by French engineers, who, having sought in vain the support of their compatriots, subsequently entered into negotiations with the British Admiralty, without success."

I do not wish to give undue publicity to certain delicate matters which once provoked considerable excitement. Yet, since all danger of injury therefrom has now come to an end, I must speak of the article that appeared in the *Echo de France*, which aroused so much comment at that time, and which threw considerable light upon the mystery of the Seven-of-Hearts. This is the article as it was published under the signature of Salvator:

THE AFFAIR OF THE SEVEN-OF-HEARTS.
A CORNER OF THE VEIL RAISED.

We will be brief. Ten years ago, a young mining engineer, Louis Lacombe, wishing to devote his time and fortune to certain studies, resigned the position he then held, and rented number 102 boulevard Maillot, a small house that had been recently built and decorated for an Italian count. Through the agency of the Varin brothers of Lausanne, one of whom assisted in the preliminary experiments and the other acted as financial agent, the young engineer was introduced to Georges Andermatt, the founder of the Metal Exchange.

After several interviews, he succeeded in interesting the banker in a submarine boat on which he was working, and it was agreed that as soon as the invention was perfected, Monsieur Andermatt would use his influence with the Minister of Marine to obtain a series of trials under the direction of the government. For two years, Louis Lacombe was a frequent visitor at Andermatt's house, and he submitted to the banker the various improvements he made upon his original plans, until one day, being satisfied with the perfection of his work, he asked Monsieur Andermatt to communicate with the Minister of Marine. That day, Louis Lacombe dined at Mon. Andermatt's house. He left there about half-past eleven at night. He has not been seen since.

A perusal of the newspapers of that date will show that the young man's family caused every possible inquiry to be made, butwithout success; and it was the general opinion that Louis Lacombe – who was known as an original and visionary youth – had quietly left for parts unknown.

Let us accept that theory – improbable, though it be – and let us consider another question, which is a most important one for our country: What has become of the plans of the submarine? Did Louis Lacombe carry them away? Are they destroyed?

After making a thorough investigation, we are able to assert, positively, that the plans are in existence, and are now in the possession of the two brothers Varin. How did they acquire such a possession? That is a question not yet determined; nor do we know why they have not tried to sell them at an earlier date. Did they fear that their title to them would be called in question? If so, they have lost that fear, and we can announce definitely, that the plans of Louis Lacombe are now the property of foreign power, and we are in a position to publish the

*correspondence that passed between the Varin brothers
and the representative of that power. The 'Seven-of-
Hearts' invented by Louis Lacombe has been actually
constructed by our neighbour.*

*Will the invention fulfil the optimistic expectations of
those who were concerned in that treacherous act?"*

And a postscript adds:

*Later – Our special correspondent informs us that
the preliminary trial of the 'Seven-of-Hearts' has not
been satisfactory. It is quite likely that the plans sold
and delivered by the Varin brothers did not include the
final document carried by Louis Lacombe to Monsieur
Andermatt on the day of his disappearance, a document
that was indispensable to a thorough understanding
of the invention. It contained a summary of the final
conclusions of the inventor, and estimates and figures
not contained in the other papers. Without this
document, the plans are incomplete; on the other hand,
without the plans, the document is worthless.*

*Now is the time to act and recover what belongs to
us. It may be a difficult matter, but we rely upon the
assistance of Monsieur Andermatt. It will be in his
interest to explain his conduct which has hitherto been
so strange and inscrutable. He should explain not only
why he concealed these facts at the time of the suicide
of Etienne Varin, but also why he has never revealed the
disappearance of the paper – a fact well known to him.
He should tell why, during the last six years, he paid
spies to watch the movements of the Varin brothers. We*

*expect from him, not only words, but acts. And at once.
Otherwise–"*

The threat was plainly expressed. But of what did it consist? What whip was Salvator, the anonymous writer of the article, holding over the head of Monsieur Andermatt?

An army of reporters attacked the banker, and ten interviewers announced the scornful manner in which they were treated. Thereupon, the *Echo de France* announced its position in these words:

"Whether Monsieur Andermatt is willing or not, he will be, henceforth, our collaborator in the work we have undertaken."

* * *

Daspry and I were dining together on the day that announcement appeared. That evening, with the newspapers spread over my table, we discussed the affair and examined it from every point of view with that exasperation that a person feels when walking in the dark and finding himself constantly falling over the same obstacles. Suddenly, without any warning whatsoever, the door opened and a lady entered. Her face was hidden behind a thick veil. I rose at once and approached her.

"Is it you, monsieur, who lives here?" she asked.

"Yes, madame, but I do not understand–"

"The gate was not locked," she explained.

"But the vestibule door?"

She did not reply, and it occurred to me that she had used the servants' entrance. How did she know the way? Then there was a silence that was quite embarrassing. She looked at Daspry, and I was obliged to introduce him. I asked her to be seated and explain the object of her visit. She raised her veil, and I saw that she was a brunette with regular features and, though not handsome, she was attractive – principally, on account of her sad, dark eyes.

"I am Madame Andermatt," she said.

"Madame Andermatt!" I repeated, with astonishment.

After a brief pause, she continued with a voice and manner that were quite easy and natural:

"I have come to see you about that affair – you know. I thought I might be able to obtain some information–"

"Mon Dieu, madame, I know nothing but what has already appeared in the papers. But if you will point out in what way I can help you ..."

"I do not know ... I do not know."

Not until then did I suspect that her calm demeanour was assumed, and that some poignant grief was concealed beneath that air of tranquillity. For a moment, we were silent and embarrassed. Then Daspry stepped forwards, and said:

"Will you permit me to ask you a few questions?"

"Yes, yes," she cried. "I will answer."

"You will answer ... whatever those questions may be?"

"Yes."

"Did you know Louis Lacombe?" he asked.

"Yes, through my husband."

"When did you see him for the last time?"

"The evening he dined with us."

"At that time, was there anything to lead you to believe that you would never see him again?"

"No. But he had spoken of a trip to Russia – in a vague way."

"Then you expected to see him again?"

"Yes. He was to dine with us two days later."

"How do you explain his disappearance?"

"I cannot explain it."

"And Monsieur. Andermatt?"

"I do not know."

"Yet the article published in the *Echo de France* indicates–"

"Yes, that the Varin brothers had something to do with his disappearance."

"Is that your opinion?"

"Yes."

"On what do you base your opinion?"

"When he left our house, Louis Lacombe carried a satchel containing all the papers relating to his invention. Two days later, my husband, in a conversation with one of the Varin brothers, learned that the papers were in their possession."

"And he did not denounce them?"

"No."

"Why not?"

"Because there was something else in the satchel— something besides the papers of Louis Lacombe."

"What was it?"

She hesitated, seemed on the verge of speaking, then finally remained silent. Daspry continued:

"I presume that is why your husband has kept a close

watch over their movements instead of informing the police. He hoped to recover the papers and, at the same time, that compromising article which has enabled the two brothers to hold over him threats of exposure and blackmail."

"Over him, and over me."

"Ah! Over you, also?"

"Over me, in particular."

She uttered the last words in a hollow voice. Daspry observed it; he paced to and fro for a moment, then, turning to her, asked:

"Had you written to Louis Lacombe?"

"Of course. My husband had business with him–"

"Apart from those business letters, had you written to Louis Lacombe ... other letters? Excuse my insistence, but it is absolutely necessary that I should know the truth. Did you write other letters?"

"Yes," she replied, blushing.

"And those letters came into the possession of the Varin brothers?"

"Yes."

"Does Monsieur Andermatt know it?"

"He has not seen them, but Alfred Varin has told him of their existence and threatened to publish them if my husband should take any steps against him. My husband was afraid ... of a scandal."

"But he has tried to recover the letters?"

"I think so; but I do not know. You see, after that last interview with Alfred Varin, and after some harsh words between me and my husband in which he called me to account – we live as strangers."

"In that case, as you have nothing to lose, what do you fear?"

"I may be indifferent to him now, but I am the woman that he has loved, the one he would still love – oh! I am quite sure of that," she murmured, in a fervent voice, "he would still love me if he had not got hold of those cursed letters–"

"What! Did he succeed? But the two brothers still defied him?"

"Yes, and they boasted of having a secure hiding place."

"Well?"

"I believe my husband discovered that hiding place."

"Ah! Where was it?"

"Here."

"Here!" I cried in alarm.

"Yes. I always had that suspicion. Louis Lacombe was very ingenious and amused himself in his leisure hours, by making safes and locks. No doubt, the Varin brothers were aware of that fact and utilized one of Lacombe's safes in which to conceal the letters ... and other things, perhaps."

"But they did not live here," I said.

"Before you came, four months ago, the house had been vacant for some time. And they may have thought that your presence here would not interfere with them when they wanted to get the papers. But they did not count on my husband, who came here on the night of the twenty-second of June, forced the safe, took what he was seeking, and left his card to inform the two brothers that he feared them no more, and that their positions were now reversed. Two days later, after reading the article in the *Gil Blas*, Etienne Varin came here, remained alone in this room, found the safe empty, and ... killed himself."

After a moment, Daspry said:

"A very simple theory ... Has Monsieur Andermatt spoken to you since then?"

"No."

"Has his attitude toward you changed in any way? Does he appear more gloomy, more anxious?"

"No, I haven't noticed any change."

"And yet you think he has secured the letters. Now, in my opinion, he has not got those letters, and it was not he who came here on the night of the twenty-second of June."

"Who was it, then?"

"The mysterious individual who is managing this affair, who holds all the threads in his hands, and whose invisible but far-reaching power we have felt from the beginning. It was he and his friends who entered this house on June twenty-second; it was he who discovered the hiding place of the papers; it was he who left Monsieur Andermatt's card; it is he who now holds the correspondence and the evidence of the treachery of the Varin brothers."

"Who is he?" I asked, impatiently.

"The man who writes letters to the *Echo de France* ... Salvator! Have we not convincing evidence of that fact? Does he not mention in his letters certain details that no one could know, except the man who had thus discovered the secrets of the two brothers?"

"Well, then," stammered Madame Andermatt, in great alarm, "he has my letters also, and it is he who now threatens my husband. Mon Dieu! What am I to do?"

"Write to him," declared Daspry. "Confide in him without reserve. Tell him all you know and all you may hereafter learn. Your interest and his interest are the same. He is not working against Monsieur Andermatt, but against Alfred Varin. Help him."

"How?"

"Has your husband the document that completes the plans of Louis Lacombe?"

"Yes."

"Tell that to Salvator, and, if possible, procure the document for him. Write to him at once. You risk nothing."

The advice was bold, dangerous even at first sight, but Madame Andermatt had no choice. Besides, as Daspry had said, she ran no risk. If the unknown writer were an enemy, that step would not aggravate the situation. If he were a stranger seeking to accomplish a particular purpose, he would attach to those letters only a secondary importance. Whatever might happen, it was the only solution offered to her, and she, in her anxiety, was only too glad to act on it. She thanked us effusively, and promised to keep us informed.

In fact, two days later, she sent us the following letter that she had received from Salvator:

Have not found the letters, but I will get them. Rest easy. I am watching everything. S.

I looked at the letter. It was in the same handwriting as the note I found in my book on the night of June the twenty-second.

Daspry was right. Salvator was, indeed, the originator of that affair.

* * *

We were beginning to see a little light coming out of the darkness that surrounded us, and an unexpected light was thrown on certain points; but other points yet remained obscure – for instance, the finding of the two seven-of-hearts. Perhaps I was unnecessarily concerned about those two cards whose seven punctured spots had appeared to me under such startling circumstances! Yet I could not refrain from asking myself: What role will they play in the drama? What importance do they bear? What conclusion must be drawn from the fact that the submarine constructed from the plans of Louis Lacombe bore the name of 'Seven-of-Hearts'?

Daspry gave little thought to the other two cards; he devoted all his attention to another problem which he considered more urgent; he was seeking the famous hiding-place.

"And who knows," said he, "I may find the letters that Salvator did not find – by inadvertence, perhaps. It is improbable that the Varin brothers would have removed from a spot which they deemed inaccessible, the weapon which was so valuable to them."

And he continued to search. In a short time, the large room held no more secrets for him, so he extended his investigations to the other rooms. He examined the interior and the exterior, the stones of the foundation, the bricks in the walls; he raised the slates of the roof.

One day, he came with a pickaxe and a spade, gave me the spade, kept the pickaxe, pointed to the adjacent vacant lots, and said: "Come."

I followed him, but I lacked his enthusiasm. He divided the vacant land into several sections which he examined in turn. At last, in a corner, at the angle formed by the walls of two neighbouring proprietors, a small pile of earth and gravel, covered with briers and grass, attracted his attention. He attacked it. I was obliged to help him. For an hour, under a hot sun, we laboured without success. I was discouraged, but Daspry urged me on. His ardour was as strong as ever.

At last, Daspry's pickaxe unearthed some bones – the remains of a skeleton to which some scraps of clothing still hung. Suddenly, I turned pale. I had discovered, sticking in the earth, a small piece of iron cut in the form of a rectangle, on which I thought I could see red spots. I stooped and picked it up. That little iron plate was the exact size of a playing-card, and the red spots, made with red lead, were arranged upon it in a manner similar to the seven-of-hearts, and each spot was pierced with a round hole similar to the perforations in the two playing cards.

"Listen, Daspry, I have had enough of this. You can stay if it interests you. But I am going."

Was that simply the expression of my excited nerves? Or was it the result of a laborious task executed under a burning sun? I know that I trembled as I walked away, and that I went to bed, where I remained forty eight hours, restless and feverish, haunted by skeletons that danced around me and threw their bleeding hearts at my head.

Daspry was faithful to me. He came to my house every day, and remained three or four hours, which he spent in the large room, ferreting, thumping, tapping.

"The letters are here, in this room," he said, from time to time, "they are here. I will stake my life on it."

On the morning of the third day, I arose – feeble yet, but cured. A substantial breakfast cheered me up. But a letter that I received that afternoon contributed, more than anything else, to my complete recovery, and aroused in me a lively curiosity. This was the letter:

Monsieur,

The drama, the first act of which transpired on the night of the twenty-second of June, is now drawing to a close. Force of circumstances compel me to bring the two principal actors in that drama face to face, and I wish that meeting to take place in your house, if you will be so kind as to give me the use of it for this evening from nine o'clock to eleven. It will be advisable to give your servant leave of absence for the evening, and perhaps you will be so kind as to leave the field open to the two adversaries. You will remember that when I visited your house on the night of June twenty-second, I took excellent care of your property. I feel that I would do you an injustice if I should doubt, for one moment, your absolute discretion in this affair. Your devoted,

SALVATOR.

I was amused at the facetious tone of his letter and also at the whimsical nature of his request. There was a charming display of confidence and candour in his language, and nothing in the world could have induced me to deceive him or repay his confidence with ingratitude.

I gave my servant a theatre ticket, and he left the house at eight o'clock. A few minutes later, Daspry arrived. I showed him the letter.

"Well?" said he.

"Well, I have left the garden gate unlocked, so anyone can enter."

"And you – are you going away?"

"Not at all. I intend to stay right here."

"But he asks you to go–"

"But I am not going. I will be discreet, but I am resolved to see what takes place."

"Ma foi!" exclaimed Daspry, laughing, "you are right, and I shall stay with you. I shouldn't like to miss it."

We were interrupted by the sound of the doorbell.

"Here already?" said Daspry, "twenty minutes ahead of time! Incredible!"

I went to the door and ushered in the visitor. It was Madame Andermatt. She was faint and nervous, and in a stammering voice, she ejaculated:

"My husband ... is coming ... he has an appointment ... they intend to give him the letters ..."

"How do you know?" I asked.

"By chance. A message came for my husband while we were at dinner. The servant gave it to me by mistake. My husband grabbed it quickly, but he was too late. I had read it."

"You read it?"

"Yes. It was something like this: 'At nine o'clock this evening, be at boulevard Maillot with the papers connected with the affair. In exchange, the letters.' So, after dinner, I hastened here."

"Unknown to your husband?"

"Yes."

"What do you think about it?" asked Daspry, turning to me.

"I think as you do, that Monsieur Andermatt is one of the invited guests."

"Yes, but for what purpose?"

"That is what we are going to find out."

I led them to a large room. The three of us could hide comfortably behind the velvet chimney mantle, and observe all that should happen in the room. We seated ourselves there, with Madame Andermatt in the centre.

The clock struck nine. A few minutes later, the garden gate creaked upon its hinges. I confess that I was greatly agitated. I was about to learn the key to the mystery. The startling events of the last few weeks were about to be explained, and, under my eyes, the last battle was going to be fought. Daspry seized the hand of Madame Andermatt, and said to her:

"Not a word, not a movement! Whatever you may see or hear, keep quiet!"

Someone entered. It was Alfred Varin. I recognized him at once, owing to the close resemblance he bore to his brother Etienne. There was the same slouching gait; the same cadaverous face covered with a black beard.

He entered with the nervous air of a man who is accustomed to fear the presence of traps and ambushes; who scents and avoids them. He glanced about the room, and I had the impression that the chimney, masked with a velvet portière, did not please him. He took three steps in our direction, when something caused him to turn and walk toward the old mosaic king, with the flowing beard and flamboyant sword, which he examined minutely, mounting on a chair and following with his fingers the outlines of the shoulders and head and feeling certain parts of the face. Suddenly, he leaped from the chair and walked away from it. He had heard the sound of approaching footsteps. Monsieur Andermatt appeared at the door.

"You! You!" exclaimed the banker. "Was it you who brought me here?"

"I? By no means," protested Varin, in a rough, jerky voice that reminded me of his brother, "on the contrary, it was your letter that brought me here."

"My letter?"

"A letter signed by you, in which you offered–"

"I never wrote to you," declared Monsieur Andermatt.

"You did not write to me!"

Instinctively, Varin was put on his guard, not against the banker, but against the unknown enemy who had drawn him into this trap. A second time, he looked in our direction, then walked toward the door. But Monsieur Andermatt barred his passage.

"Well, where are you going, Varin?"

"There is something about this affair I don't like. I am going home. Good evening."

"One moment!"

"No need of that, Monsieur Andermatt. I have nothing to say to you."

"But I have something to say to you, and this is a good time to say it."

"Let me pass."

"No, you will not pass."

Varin recoiled before the resolute attitude of the banker, as he muttered:

"Well, then, be quick about it."

One thing astonished me; and I have no doubt my two companions experienced a similar feeling. Why was Salvator not there? Was he not a necessary party at this conference? Or was he satisfied to let these two adversaries fight it out between themselves? At all events, his absence was a great disappointment, although it did not detract from the dramatic strength of the situation.

After a moment, Monsieur Andermatt approached Varin and, face to face, eye to eye, said:

"Now, after all these years and when you have nothing more to fear, you can answer me candidly: What have you done with Louis Lacombe?"

"What a question! As if I knew anything about him!"

"You do know! You and your brother were his constant companions, almost lived with him in this very house. You knew all about his plans and his work. And the last night I ever saw Louis Lacombe, when I parted with him at my door, I saw two men slinking away in the shadows of the trees. That, I am ready to swear to."

"Well, what has that to do with me?"

"The two men were you and your brother."

"Prove it."

"The best proof is that, two days later, you yourself showed me the papers and the plans that belonged to Lacombe and offered to sell them. How did these papers come into your possession?"

"I have already told you, Monsieur Andermatt, that we found them on Louis Lacombe's table, the morning after his disappearance."

"That is a lie!"

"Prove it."

"The law will prove it."

"Why did you not appeal to the law?"

"Why? Ah! Why–," stammered the banker, with a slight display of emotion.

"You know very well, Monsieur Andermatt, if you had the least certainty of our guilt, our little threat would not have stopped you."

"What threat? Those letters? Do you suppose I ever gave those letters a moment's thought?"

"If you did not care for the letters, why did you offer me thousands of francs for their return? And why did you have my brother and me tracked like wild beasts?"

"To recover the plans."

"Nonsense! You wanted the letters. You knew that as soon as you had the letters in your possession, you could denounce us. Oh! no, I couldn't part with them!"

He laughed heartily, but stopped suddenly, and said:

"But, enough of this! We are merely going over old ground. We make no headway. We had better let things stand as they are."

"We will not let them stand as they are," said the banker, "and since you have referred to the letters, let me tell you that you will not leave this house until you deliver up those letters."

"I shall go when I please."

"You will not."

"Be careful, Monsieur Andermatt. I warn you–"

"I say, you shall not go."

"We will see about that," cried Varin, in such a rage that Madame Andermatt could not suppress a cry of fear. Varin must have heard it, for he now tried to force his way out. Monsieur Andermatt pushed him back. Then I saw him put his hand into his coat pocket.

"For the last time, let me pass!" he cried.

"The letters, first!"

Varin drew a revolver and, pointing it at Monsieur Andermatt, said:

"Yes or no?"

The banker stooped quickly. There was the sound of a pistol shot. The weapon fell from Varin's hand. I was amazed. The shot was fired close to me. It was Daspry who had fired it at Varin, causing him to drop the revolver. In a moment, Daspry was standing between the two men, facing Varin; he said to him, with a sneer:

"You were lucky, my friend, very lucky. I fired at your hand and struck only the revolver."

Both of them looked at him, surprised. Then he turned to the banker, and said:

"I beg your pardon, monsieur, for meddling in your business; but, really, you play a very poor game. Let me hold the cards."

Turning again to Varin, Daspry said:

"It's between us two, comrade, and play fair, if you please. Hearts are trumps, and I play the seven."

Then Daspry held up, before Varin's bewildered eyes, the little iron plate, marked with the seven red spots. It was a terrible shock to Varin. With livid features, staring eyes, and an air of intense agony, the man seemed to be hypnotized at the sight of it.

"Who are you?" he gasped.

"One who meddles in other people's business, down to the very bottom."

"What do you want?"

"What you brought here tonight."

"I brought nothing."

"Yes, you did, or you wouldn't have come. This morning, you received an invitation to come here at nine o'clock, and bring with you all the papers held by you. You are here. Where are the papers?"

There was in Daspry's voice and manner a tone of authority that I did not understand; his manner was usually quite mild and conciliatory. Absolutely conquered, Varin placed his hand on one of his pockets, and said:

"The papers are here."

"All of them?"

"Yes."

"All that you took from Louis Lacombe and afterwards sold to Major von Lieben?"

"Yes."

"Are these the copies or the originals?"

"I have the originals."

"How much do you want for them?"

"One hundred thousand francs."

"You are crazy," said Daspry. "Why, the major gave you only twenty thousand, and that was like money thrown into the sea, as the boat was a failure at the preliminary trials."

"They didn't understand the plans."

"The plans are not complete."

"Then, why do you ask me for them?"

"Because I want them. I offer you five thousand francs – not a sou more."

"Ten thousand. Not a sou less."

"Agreed," said Daspry, who now turned to Monsieur Andermatt, and said:

"Monsieur will kindly sign a cheque for the amount."

"But ... I haven't got–"

"Your chequebook? Here it is."

Astounded, Monsieur Andermatt examined the chequebook that Daspry handed to him.

"It is mine," he gasped. "How did you do that?"

"No idle words, monsieur, if you please. You have merely to sign."

The banker took out his fountain pen, filled out the check and signed it. Varin held out his hand for it.

"Put down your hand," said Daspry, "there is something more." Then, to the banker, he said: "You asked for some letters, did you not?"

"Yes, a package of letters."

"Where are they, Varin?"

"I haven't got them."

"Where are they, Varin?"

"I don't know. My brother had charge of them."

"They are hidden in this room."

"In that case, you know where they are."

"How should I know?"

"Was it not you who found the hiding-place? You appear to be as well informed ... as Salvator."

"The letters are not in the hiding-place."

"They are."

"Open it."

Varin looked at him, defiantly. Were not Daspry and Salvator the same person? Everything pointed to that conclusion. If so, Varin risked nothing in disclosing a hiding place already known.

"Open it," repeated Daspry.

"I have not got the seven of hearts."

"Yes, here it is," said Daspry, handing him the iron plate. Varin recoiled in terror, and cried:

"No, no, I will not."

"Never mind," replied Daspry, as he walked toward the bearded king, climbed on a chair and applied the seven of hearts to the lower part of the sword in such a manner that the edges of the iron plate coincided exactly with the two edges of the sword. Then, with the assistance of an awl which he introduced alternately into each of the seven holes, he pressed upon seven of the little mosaic stones. As he pressed upon the seventh one, a clicking sound was heard, and the entire bust of the King turned upon a pivot, disclosing a large opening lined with steel. It was really a fire-proof safe.

"You can see, Varin, the safe is empty."

"So I see. Then, my brother has taken out the letters."

Daspry stepped down from the chair, approached Varin, and said:

"Now, no more nonsense with me. There is another hiding place. Where is it?"

"There is none."

"Is it money you want? How much?"

"Ten thousand."

"Monsieur Andermatt, are those letters worth ten thousand francs to you?"

"Yes," said the banker, firmly.

Varin closed the safe, took the seven of hearts and placed it again on the sword at the same spot. He thrust the awl into each of the seven holes. There was the same clicking sound, but this time, strange to relate, it was only a portion of the safe that revolved on the pivot, disclosing quite a small safe that was built within the door of the larger one. The packet of letters was here, tied with a tape, and sealed. Varin handed the packet to Daspry. The latter turned to the banker, and asked:

"Is the check ready, Monsieur Andermatt?"

"Yes."

"And you have also the last document that you received from Louis Lacombe – the one that completes the plans of the submarine?"

"Yes."

The exchange was made. Daspry pocketed the document and the checks, and offered the packet of letters to Monsieur Andermatt.

"This is what you wanted, Monsieur."

The banker hesitated a moment, as if he were afraid to touch those cursed letters that he had sought so eagerly. Then, with a nervous movement, he took them. Close to me, I heard a moan. I grasped Madame Andermatt's hand. It was cold.

"I believe, monsieur," said Daspry to the banker, "that our business is ended. Oh! No thanks. It was only by a mere chance that I have been able to do you a good turn. Goodnight."

Monsieur Andermatt retired. He carried with him the letters written by his wife to Louis Lacombe.

"Marvellous!" exclaimed Daspry, delighted. "Everything is coming our way. Now, we have only to close our little affair, comrade. You have the papers?"

"Here they are – all of them."

Daspry examined them carefully, and then placed them in his pocket.

"Quite right. You have kept your word," he said.

"But–"

"But what?"

"The two cheques? The money?" said Varin, eagerly.

"Well, you have a great deal of assurance, my man. How dare you ask such a thing?"

"I ask only what is due to me."

"Can you ask pay for returning papers that you stole? Well, I think not!"

Varin was beside himself. He trembled with rage; his eyes were bloodshot.

"The money ... the twenty thousand ..." he stammered.

"Impossible! I need it myself."

"The money!"

"Come, be reasonable, and don't get excited. It won't do you any good."

Daspry seized his arm so forcibly, that Varin uttered a cry of pain. Daspry continued:

"Now, you can go. The air will do you good. Perhaps you want me to show you the way. Ah! Yes, we will go together to the vacant lot near here, and I will show you a little mound of earth and stones and under it–"

"That is false! That is false!"

"Oh! No, it is true. That little iron plate with the seven spots on it came from there. Louis Lacombe always carried it, and you buried it with the body – and with some other things that will prove very interesting to a judge and jury."

Varin covered his face with his hands, and muttered:

"All right, I am beaten. Say no more. But I want to ask you one question. I should like to know–"

"What is it?"

"Was there a little casket in the large safe?"

"Yes."

"Was it there on the night of the twenty-second of June?"

"Yes."

"What did it contain?"

"Everything that the Varin brothers had put in it – a very pretty collection of diamonds and pearls picked up here and there by the said brothers."

"And did you take it?"

"Of course I did. Do you blame me?"

"I understand ... it was the disappearance of that casket that caused my brother to kill himself."

"Probably. The disappearance of your correspondence was not a sufficient motive. But the disappearance of the casket ... Is that all you wish to ask me?"

"One thing more: your name?"

"You ask that with an idea of seeking revenge."

"Parbleu! The tables may be turned. Today, you are on top. Tomorrow–"

"It will be you."

"I hope so. Your name?"

"Arsène Lupin."

"Arsène Lupin!"

The man staggered, as though stunned by a heavy blow. Those two words had deprived him of all hope.

Daspry laughed, and said:

"Ah! Did you imagine that a Monsieur Durand or Dupont could manage an affair like this? No, it required the skill and cunning of Arsène Lupin. And now that you have my name, go and prepare your revenge. Arsène Lupin will wait for you."

Then he pushed the bewildered Varin through the door.

"Daspry! Daspry!" I cried, pushing aside the curtain. He ran to me.

"What? What's the matter?"

"Madame Andermatt is ill."

He hastened to her, caused her to inhale some salts, and, while caring for her, questioned me:

"Well, what did it?"

"The letters of Louis Lacombe that you gave to her husband."

He struck his forehead and said:

"Did she think that I could do such a thing! But, of course she would. Imbecile that I am!"

Madame Andermatt was now revived. Daspry took from his pocket a small package exactly similar to the one that Monsieur Andermatt had carried away.

"Here are your letters, Madame. These are the genuine letters."

"But ... the others?"

"The others are the same, rewritten by me and carefully

worded. Your husband will not find anything objectionable in them, and will never suspect the substitution since they were taken from the safe in his presence."

"But the handwriting–"

"There is no handwriting that cannot be imitated."

She thanked him in the same words she might have used to a man in her own social circle, so I concluded that she had not witnessed the final scene between Varin and Arsène Lupin. But the surprising revelation caused me considerable embarrassment. Lupin! My club companion was none other than Arsène Lupin. I could not realize it. But he said, quite at his ease:

"You can say farewell to Jean Daspry."

"Ah!"

"Yes, Jean Daspry is going on a long journey. I shall send him to Morocco. There, he may find a death worthy of him. I may say that that is his expectation."

"But Arsène Lupin will remain?"

"Oh! Decidedly. Arsène Lupin is simply at the threshold of his career, and he expects–"

I was impelled by curiosity to interrupt him, and, leading him away from the hearing of Madame Andermatt, I asked:

"Did you discover the smaller safe yourself – the one that held the letters?"

"Yes, after a great deal of trouble. I found it yesterday afternoon while you were asleep. And yet, God knows it was simple enough! But the simplest things are the ones that usually escape our notice." Then, showing me the seven-of-hearts, he added: "Of course I had guessed that, in order to open the larger safe, this card must be placed on the sword of the mosaic king."

"How did you guess that?"

"Quite easily. Through private information, I knew that fact when I came here on the evening of the twenty-second of June–"

"After you left me–"

"Yes, after turning the subject of our conversation to stories of crime and robbery which were sure to reduce you to such a nervous condition that you would not leave your bed, but would allow me to complete my search uninterrupted."

"The scheme worked perfectly."

"Well, I knew when I came here that there was a casket concealed in a safe with a secret lock, and that the seven-of-hearts was the key to that lock. I had merely to place the card upon the spot that was obviously intended for it. An hour's examination showed me where the spot was."

"One hour!"

"Observe the fellow in mosaic."

"The old emperor?"

"That old emperor is an exact representation of the king of hearts on all playing cards."

"That's right. But how does the seven of hearts open the larger safe at one time and the smaller safe at another time? And why did you open only the larger safe in the first instance? I mean on the night of the twenty-second of June."

"Why? Because I always placed the seven of hearts in the same way. I never changed the position. But, yesterday, I observed that by reversing the card, by turning it upside down, the arrangement of the seven spots on the mosaic was changed."

"Parbleu!"

"Of course, parbleu! But a person has to think of those things."

"There is something else: you did not know the history of those letters until Madame Andermatt—"

"Spoke of them before me? No. Because I found in the safe, besides the casket, nothing but the correspondence of the two brothers which disclosed their treachery in regard to the plans."

"Then it was by chance that you were led, first, to investigate the history of the two brothers, and then to search for the plans and documents relating to the submarine?"

"Simply by chance."

"For what purpose did you make the search?"

"Mon Dieu!" exclaimed Daspry, laughing, "how deeply interested you are!"

"The subject fascinates me."

"Very well, presently, after I have escorted Madame Andermatt to a carriage, and dispatched a short story to the *Echo de France,* I will return and tell you all about it."

He sat down and wrote one of those short, clear-cut articles which served to amuse and mystify the public. Who does not recall the sensation that followed that article produced throughout the entire world?

"Arsène Lupin has solved the problem recently submitted by Salvator. Having acquired possession of all the documents and original plans of the engineer Louis Lacombe, he has placed them in the hands of the Minister of Marine Affairs, and he has headed a subscription list for the purpose of presenting to the nation the first submarine constructed from those plans. His subscription is twenty thousand francs."

"Twenty thousand francs! The checks of Monsieur Andermatt?" I exclaimed, when he had given me the paper to read.

"Exactly. It was quite right that Varin should redeem his treachery."

* * *

And that is how I made the acquaintance of Arsène Lupin. That is how I learned that Jean Daspry, a member of my club, was none other than Arsène Lupin, gentleman-thief. That is how I formed very agreeable ties of friendship with that famous man, and, thanks to the confidence with which he honoured me, how I became his very humble and faithful historiographer.

MADAME
IMBERT'S SAFE

At three o'clock in the morning, there were still half a dozen carriages in front of one of those small houses which form only the side of the boulevard Berthier. The door of that house opened, and a number of guests, male and female, emerged. The majority of them entered their carriages and were quickly driven away, leaving behind only two men who walked down Courcelles, where they parted, as one of them lived in that street. The other decided to return on foot as far as the Porte-Maillot. It was a beautiful winter's night, clear and cold; a night on which a brisk walk is agreeable and refreshing.

But, at the end of a few minutes, he had the disagreeable impression that he was being followed. Turning around, he saw a man skulking amongst the trees. He was not a coward; yet he felt it advisable to increase his speed. Then his pursuer commenced to run; and he deemed it prudent to draw his revolver and face him. But he had no time. The man rushed at him and attacked him violently. Immediately, they were engaged in a desperate struggle, wherein he felt that his unknown assailant had the advantage. He called for help, struggled, and was thrown down on a pile of gravel, seized by the throat, and gagged with a handkerchief that his assailant forced into his mouth. His eyes closed, and the man who was smothering him with his weight arose to defend himself against an unexpected attack. A blow from a cane and a kick from a boot; the man uttered two cries of pain, and fled, limping and cursing. Without deigning to pursue the fugitive, the new arrival stooped over the prostrate man and enquired:

"Are you hurt, monsieur?"

He was not injured, but he was dazed and unable to stand. His rescuer procured a carriage, placed him in it, and accompanied him to his house on the avenue de la Grande-Armée. On his arrival there, quite recovered, he overwhelmed his saviour with thanks.

"I owe you my life, monsieur, and I shall not forget it. I do not wish to alarm my wife at this time of night, but, tomorrow, she will be pleased to thank you personally. Come and breakfast with us. My name is Ludovic Imbert. May I ask yours?"

"Certainly, monsieur."

And he handed Monsieur Imbert a card bearing the name: "Arsène Lupin."

* * *

At that time, Arsène Lupin did not enjoy the celebrity which the Cahorn affair, his escape from the Prison de la Santé, and other brilliant exploits, afterwards gained for him.

He had never even used the name of Arsène Lupin. The name was specially invented to designate the rescuer of Monsieur Imbert; that is to say, it was in this affair that Arsène Lupin was baptized. Fully armed and ready for the fray, it is true, but lacking the resources and authority which command success, Arsène Lupin was then merely an apprentice in a profession wherein he soon became a master.

With what a thrill of joy he recalled the invitation he received that night! At last, he had reached his goal! At last, he had undertaken a task worthy of his strength and skill! The Imbert millions! What a magnificent feast for an appetite like his!

He prepared a special outfit for the occasion; a shabby frock coat, baggy trousers, a frayed silk hat, well-worn collar and cuffs, all quite correct in form, but bearing the unmistakable stamp of poverty. His cravat was a black ribbon pinned with a false diamond. Thus accoutred, he descended the stairs of the house in which he lived at Montmartre. At the third floor, without stopping, he rapped on a closed door with the head of his cane. He walked to the exterior boulevards. A tram car was passing. He boarded it, and someone who had been following him took a seat beside him. It was the lodger who occupied the room on the third floor. A moment later, this man said to Lupin:

"Well, governor?"

"Well, it is all fixed."

"How?"

"I am going there to breakfast."

"You breakfast – there!"

"Certainly. Why not? I rescued Monsieur Ludovic Imbert from certain death at your hands. Monsieur Imbert is not devoid of gratitude. He invited me to breakfast."

There was a brief silence. Then the other said:

"But you are not going to throw up the scheme?"

"My dear boy," said Lupin, "When I arranged that little case of assault and battery, when I took the trouble at three o'clock in the morning, to rap you with my cane and tap you with my boot at the risk of injuring my only friend, it was not my intention to forego the advantages to be gained from a rescue so well arranged and executed. Oh! No, not at all."

"But the strange rumours we hear about their fortune?"

"Never mind about that. For six months, I have worked on this affair, investigated it, studied it, questioned the servants, the moneylenders and men of straw; for six months, I have shadowed the husband and wife. Consequently, I know what I am talking about. Whether the fortune came to them from old Brawford, as they pretend, or from some other source, I do not care. I know that it is a reality; that it exists. And some day it will be mine."

"Bigre! One hundred million!"

"Let us say ten, or even five – that is enough! They have a safe full of bonds, and there will be the devil to pay if I can't get my hands on them."

The tram car stopped at the place de l'Etoile. The man whispered to Lupin:

"What am I to do now?"

"Nothing, at present. You will hear from me. There is no hurry."

Five minutes later, Arsène Lupin was ascending the magnificent flight of stairs in the Imbert mansion, and Monsieur Imbert introduced him to his wife. Madame Gervaise Imbert was a short plump woman, and very talkative. She gave Lupin a cordial welcome.

"I desired that we should be alone to entertain our saviour," she said.

From the outset, they treated 'our saviour' as an old and valued friend. By the time dessert was served, their friendship was well cemented, and private confidences were being exchanged. Arsène related the story of his life, the life of his father as a magistrate, the sorrows of his childhood, and his present difficulties. Gervaise, in turn, spoke of her youth, her marriage, the kindness of the aged Brawford, the hundred millions that she had inherited, the obstacles that prevented her from obtaining the enjoyment of her inheritance, the moneys she had been obliged to borrow at an exorbitant rate of interest, her endless contentions with Brawford's nephews, and the litigation! The injunctions! In fact, everything!

"Just think of it, Monsieur Lupin, the bonds are there in my husband's office, and if we detach a single coupon, we lose everything! They are there, in our safe, and we dare not touch them."

Monsieur Lupin shivered at the bare idea of his proximity to so much wealth. Yet he felt quite certain that Monsieur Lupin would never suffer from the same difficulty as his fair hostess who declared she dare not touch the money.

"Ah! They are there!" he repeated, to himself; "they are there!"

A friendship formed under such circumstances soon led to closer relations. When discreetly questioned, Arsène Lupin confessed his poverty and distress. Immediately, the unfortunate young man was appointed private secretary to the Imberts, husband and wife, at a salary of one hundred francs a month. He was to come to the house every day and receive orders for his work, and a room on the second floor was set apart as his office. This room was directly over Monsieur Imbert's office.

Arsène soon realized that his position as secretary was essentially a sinecure. During the first two months, he had only four important letters to recopy, and was called only once to Monsieur Imbert's office; consequently, he had only one opportunity to contemplate, officially, the Imbert safe. Moreover, he noticed that the secretary was not invited to the social functions of the employer. But he did not complain, as he preferred to remain, modestly, in the shade and maintain his peace and freedom.

However, he was not wasting any time. From the beginning, he made clandestine visits to Monsieur Imbert's office, and paid his respects to the safe, which was hermetically closed. It was an immense block of iron and steel, cold and stern in appearance, which could not be forced open by the ordinary tools of the burglar's trade. But Arsène Lupin was not discouraged.

"Where force fails, cunning prevails," he said to himself. "The essential thing is to be on the spot when the opportunity occurs. In the meantime, I must watch and wait."

He made immediately some preliminary preparations. After careful soundings made upon the floor of his room, he introduced a lead pipe which penetrated the ceiling of Monsieur Imbert's office at a point between the two screeds of the cornice. By means of this pipe, he hoped to see and hear what transpired in the room below.

Henceforth, he passed his days stretched at full length upon the floor. He frequently saw the Imberts holding a consultation in front of the safe, investigating books and papers. When they turned the combination lock, he tried to learn the figures and the number of turns they made to the right and left. He watched their movements; he sought to catch their words. There was also a key necessary to complete the opening of the safe. What did they do with it? Did they hide it?

One day, he saw them leave the room without locking the safe. He descended the stairs quickly, and boldly entered the room. But they had returned.

"Oh! excuse me," he said, "I opened the wrong door."

"Come in, Monsieur Lupin, come in," cried Madame Imbert, "are you not at home here? We want your advice. What bonds should we sell? The foreign securities or the government annuities?"

"But the injunction?" said Lupin, with surprise.

"Oh! it doesn't cover all the bonds."

She opened the door of the safe and withdrew a package of bonds. But her husband protested.

"No, no, Gervaise, it would be foolish to sell the foreign bonds. They are going up, whilst the annuities are as high as they ever will be. What do you think, my dear friend?"

The dear friend had no opinion; yet he advised the sacrifice of the annuities. Then she withdrew another package and, from it, she took a paper at random. It proved to be a three percent annuity worth two thousand francs. Ludovic placed the package of bonds in his pocket. That afternoon, accompanied by his secretary, he sold the annuities to a stock-broker and realized forty-six thousand francs.

Whatever Madame Imbert might have said about it, Arsène Lupin did not feel at home in the Imbert house. On the contrary, his position there was a peculiar one. He learned that the servants did not even know his name. They called him 'monsieur.' Ludovic always spoke of him in the same way: "You will tell monsieur. Has monsieur arrived?" Why that mysterious appellation?

Moreover, after their first outburst of enthusiasm, the Imberts seldom spoke to him, and, although treating him with the consideration due to a benefactor, they gave him little or no attention. They appeared to regard him as an eccentric character who did not like to be disturbed, and they respected his isolation as if it were a stringent rule on his part. On one occasion, while passing through the vestibule, he heard Madame Imbert say to the two gentlemen:

"He is such a barbarian!"

"Very well," he said to himself, "I am a barbarian."

And, without seeking to solve the question of their strange conduct, he proceeded with the execution of his own plans. He had decided that he could not depend on chance, nor on the negligence of Madame Imbert, who carried the key of the safe, and who, on locking the safe, invariably scattered the letters forming the combination of the lock. Consequently, he must act for himself.

Finally, an incident precipitated matters; it was the vehement campaign instituted against the Imberts by certain newspapers that accused the Imberts of swindling. Arsène Lupin was present at certain family conferences when this new vicissitude was discussed. He decided that if he waited much longer, he would lose everything. During the next five days, instead of leaving the house about six o'clock, according to his usual habit, he locked himself in his room. It was supposed that he had gone out. But he was lying on the floor surveying the office of Monsieur Imbert. During those five evenings, the favourable opportunity that he awaited did not take place. He left the house about midnight by a side door to which he held the key.

But on the sixth day, he learned that the Imberts, actuated by the malevolent insinuations of their enemies, proposed to make an inventory of the contents of the safe.

"They will do it tonight," thought Lupin.

And truly, after dinner, Imbert and his wife retired to the office and commenced to examine the books of account and the securities contained in the safe. Thus, one hour after another passed away. He heard the servants go upstairs to their rooms. No one now remained on the first floor. Midnight! The Imberts were still at work.

"I must get to work," murmured Lupin.

He opened his window. It opened on a court. Outside, everything was dark and quiet. He took from his desk a knotted rope, fastened it to the balcony in front of his window, and quietly descended as far as the window below, which was that of the of Imbert's office. He stood upon the balcony for a moment, motionless, with attentive ear and watchful eye, but the heavy curtains effectually concealed the interior of the room. He cautiously pushed on the double window. If no one had examined it, it ought to yield to the slightest pressure, for, during the afternoon, he had so fixed the bolt that it would not enter the staple.

The window yielded to his touch. Then, with infinite care, he pushed it open sufficiently to admit his head. He parted the curtains a few inches, looked in, and saw Monsieur Imbert and his wife sitting in front of the safe, deeply absorbed in their work and speaking softly to each other at rare intervals.

He calculated the distance between him and them, considered the exact movements he would require to make in order to overcome them, one after the other, before they could call for help, and he was about to rush upon them, when Madame Imbert said:

"Ah! The room is getting quite cold. I am going to bed. And you, my dear?"

"I shall stay and finish."

"Finish! Why, that will take you all night."

"Not at all. An hour, at the most."

She retired. Twenty minutes, thirty minutes passed. Arsène pushed the window a little farther open. The curtains shook. He pushed once more. Monsieur Imbert turned, and, seeing the curtains blown by the wind, he rose to close the window.

There was not a cry, not the trace of struggle. With a few precise movements, and without causing him the least injury, Arsène stunned him, wrapped the curtain about his head, bound him hand and foot, and did it all in such a manner that Monsieur Imbert had no opportunity to recognize his assailant.

Quickly, he approached the safe, seized two packages that he placed under his arm, left the office, and opened the servants' gate. A carriage was stationed in the street.

"Take that, first – and follow me," he said to the coachman. He returned to the office, and, in two trips, they emptied the safe. Then Arsène went to his own room, removed the rope, and all other traces of his clandestine work.

A few hours later, Arsène Lupin and his assistant examined the stolen goods. Lupin was not disappointed, as he had foreseen that the wealth of the Imberts had been greatly exaggerated. It did not consist of hundreds of millions, nor even tens of millions. Yet it amounted to a very respectable sum, and Lupin expressed his satisfaction.

"Of course," he said, "there will be a considerable loss when we come to sell the bonds, as we will have to dispose of them surreptitiously at reduced prices. In the meantime, they will rest quietly in my desk awaiting a propitious moment."

Arsène saw no reason why he should not go to the Imbert house the next day. But a perusal of the morning papers revealed this startling fact: Ludovic and Gervaise Imbert had disappeared.

When the officers of the law seized the safe and opened it, they found there what Arsène Lupin had left – nothing.

* * *

Such are the facts; and I learned the sequel to them, one day, when Arsène Lupin was in a confidential mood. He was pacing to and fro in my room, with a nervous step and a feverish eye that were unusual to him.

"After all," I said to him, "it was your most successful venture."

Without making a direct reply, he said:

"There are some impenetrable secrets connected with that affair; some obscure points that escape my comprehension. For instance: What caused their flight? Why did they not take advantage of the help I unconsciously gave them? It would have been so simple to say: 'The hundred million was in the safe. They are no longer there, because they have been stolen.'"

"They lost their nerve."

"Yes, that is it – they lost their nerve ... On the other hand, it is true–"

"What is true?"

"Oh! Nothing."

What was the meaning of Lupin's reticence? It was quite obvious that he had not told me everything; there was something he was loath to tell. His conduct puzzled me. It must indeed be a very serious matter to cause such a man as Arsène Lupin even a momentary hesitation. I threw out a few questions at random.

"Have you seen them since?"

"No."

"And have you never experienced the slightest degree of pity for those unfortunate people?"

"I!" he exclaimed, with a start.

His sudden excitement astonished me. Had I touched him on a sore spot? I continued:

"Of course. If you had not left them alone, they might have been able to face the danger, or, at least, made their escape with full pockets."

"What do you mean?" he said, indignantly. "I suppose you have an idea that my soul should be filled with remorse?"

"Call it remorse or regrets – anything you like–"

"They are not worth it."

"Have you no regrets or remorse for having stolen their fortune?"

"What fortune?"

"The packages of bonds you took from their safe."

"Oh! I stole their bonds, did I? I deprived them of a portion of their wealth? Is that my crime? Ah! My dear boy, you do not know the truth. You never imagined that those bonds were not worth the paper they were written on. Those bonds were false – they were counterfeit – every one of them – do you understand? **THEY WERE COUNTERFEIT!**"

I looked at him, astounded.

"Counterfeit! The four or five million?"

"Yes, counterfeit!" he exclaimed, in a fit of rage. "Only so many scraps of paper! I couldn't raise a sou on the whole of them! And you ask me if I have any remorse. They are the ones who should have remorse and pity. They played me for a simpleton; and I fell into their trap.

I was their latest victim, their most stupid gull!"

He was affected by genuine anger – the result of malice and wounded pride. He continued:

"From start to finish, I got the worst of it. Do you know the part I played in that affair, or rather the part they made me play? That of André Brawford! Yes, my boy, that is the truth, and I never suspected it. It was not until afterwards, on reading the newspapers, that the light finally dawned in my stupid brain. Whilst I was posing as his 'saviour', as the gentleman who had risked his life to rescue Monsieur Imbert from the clutches of an assassin, they were passing me off as Brawford. Wasn't that splendid? That eccentric individual who had a room on the second floor, that barbarian that was exhibited only at a distance, was Brawford, and Brawford was I! Thanks to me, and to the confidence that I inspired under the name of Brawford, they were enabled to borrow money from the bankers and other moneylenders. Ha! What an experience for a novice! And I swear to you that I shall profit by the lesson!"

He stopped, seized my arm, and said to me, in a tone of exasperation:

"My dear fellow, at this very moment, Gervaise Imbert owes me fifteen hundred francs."

I could not refrain from laughter, his rage was so grotesque. He was making a mountain out of a molehill. In a moment, he laughed himself, and said:

"Yes, my boy, fifteen hundred francs. You must know that I had not received one sou of my promised salary, and, more than that, she had borrowed from me the sum of fifteen hundred francs. All my youthful savings! And do you know why? To devote the money to charity! I am giving you a straight story. She wanted it for some poor people she was assisting – unknown to her husband. And my hard-earned money was wormed out of me by that silly pretence! Isn't it amusing, hein? Arsène Lupin done out of fifteen hundred francs by the fair lady from whom he stole four millions in counterfeit bonds! And what a vast amount of time and patience and cunning I expended to achieve that result! It was the first time in my life that I was played for a fool, and I frankly confess that I was fooled that time to the queen's taste!"

THE
BLACK PEARL

A violent ringing of the bell awakened the concierge of number nine, avenue Hoche. She pulled the door string, grumbling:

"I thought everybody was in. It must be three o'clock!"

"Perhaps it is someone for the doctor," muttered her husband.

At that moment, a voice enquired:

"Doctor Harel ... what floor?"

"Third floor, left. But the doctor won't go out at night."

"He must go tonight."

The visitor entered the vestibule, ascended to the first floor, the second, the third, and, without stopping at the doctor's door, he continued to the fifth floor. There, he tried two keys. One of them fitted the lock.

"Ah! Good!" he murmured, "that simplifies the business wonderfully. But before I commence work I had better arrange for my retreat. Let me see ... have I had sufficient time to rouse the doctor and be dismissed by him? Not yet ... a few minutes more."

At the end of ten minutes, he descended the stairs, grumbling noisily about the doctor. The concierge opened the door for him and heard it click behind him. But the door did not lock, as the man had quickly inserted a piece of iron in the lock in such a manner that the bolt could not enter. Then, quietly, he entered the house again, unknown to the concierge. In case of alarm, his retreat was assured. Noiselessly, he ascended to the fifth floor once more. In the antechamber, by the light of his electric lantern, he placed his hat and overcoat on one of the chairs, took a seat on another, and covered his heavy shoes with felt slippers.

"Ouf! Here I am – and how simple it was! I wonder why more people do not adopt the profitable and pleasant occupation of burglar. With a little care and reflection, it becomes a most delightful profession. Not too quiet and monotonous, of course, as it would then become wearisome."

He unfolded a detailed plan of the apartment.

"Let me commence by locating myself. Here, I see the vestibule in which I am sitting. On the street front, the drawing room, the boudoir and dining room. Useless to waste any time there, as it appears that the countess has a deplorable taste ... not a bibelot of any value! Now, let's get down to business! Ah! Here is a corridor; it must lead to the bed chambers. At a distance of three metres, I should come to the door of the wardrobe-closet which connects with the chamber of the countess." He folded his plan, extinguished his lantern, and proceeded down the corridor, counting his distance, thus:

"One metre ... two metres ... three metres ... Here

is the door ... Mon Dieu, how easy it is! Only a small, simple bolt now separates me from the chamber, and I know that the bolt is located exactly one metre, forty-three centimetres, from the floor. So that, thanks to a small incision I am about to make, I can soon get rid of the bolt."

He drew from his pocket the necessary instruments. Then the following idea occurred to him:

"Suppose, by chance, the door is not bolted. I will try it first."

He turned the knob, and the door opened.

"My brave Lupin, surely fortune favours you ... What's to be done now? You know the situation of the rooms; you know the place in which the countess hides the black pearl. Therefore, in order to secure the black pearl, you have simply to be more silent than silence, more invisible than darkness itself."

Arsène Lupin was employed fully a half-hour in opening the second door – a glass door that led to the countess' bedchamber. But he accomplished it with so much skill and precaution, that even had the countess been awake, she would not have heard the slightest sound. According to the plan of the rooms, that he held, he had merely to pass around a reclining chair and, beyond that, a small table close to the bed. On the table, there was a box of letter paper, and the black pearl was concealed in that box. He stooped and crept cautiously over the carpet, following the outlines of the reclining-chair. When he reached the extremity of it, he stopped in order to repress the throbbing of his heart. Although he was not moved by any sense of fear, he found it impossible to overcome the nervous anxiety that one usually feels in the midst of profound silence. That circumstance astonished him, because he had passed through many more solemn moments without the slightest trace of emotion. No danger threatened him. Then why did his heart throb like an alarm bell? Was it that sleeping woman who affected him? Was it the proximity of another pulsating heart?

He listened, and thought he could discern the rhythmical breathing of a person asleep. It gave him confidence, like the presence of a friend. He sought and found the armchair; then, by slow, cautious movements, advanced toward the table, feeling ahead of him with outstretched arm. His right had touched one of the feet of the table. Ah! Now, he had simply to rise, take the pearl, and escape. That was fortunate, as his heart was leaping in his breast like a wild beast, and made so much noise that he feared it would wake the countess. By a powerful effort of the will, he subdued the wild throbbing of his heart, and was about to rise from the floor when his left hand encountered, lying on the floor, an object which he recognized as a candlestick – an overturned candlestick. A moment later, his hand encountered another object: a clock – one of those small travelling clocks, covered with leather.

Well! What had happened? He could not understand. That candlestick, that clock; why were those articles not in their accustomed places? Ah! What had happened in the dread silence of the night?

Suddenly a cry escaped him. He had touched – oh! Some strange, unutterable thing! "No! no!" he thought, "it cannot be. It is some fantasy of my excited brain." For twenty seconds, thirty seconds, he remained motionless, terrified, his forehead bathed with perspiration, and his fingers still retained the sensation of that dreadful contact.

Making a desperate effort, he ventured to extend his arm again. Once more, his hand encountered that strange, unutterable thing. He felt it. He must feel it and find out what it is. He found that it was hair, human hair, and a human face; and that face was cold, almost icy.

However frightful the circumstances may be, a man like Arsène Lupin controls himself and commands the situation as soon as he learns what it is. So, Arsène Lupin quickly brought his lantern into use. A woman was lying before him, covered with blood. Her neck and shoulders were covered with gaping wounds. He leaned over her and made a closer examination. She was dead.

"Dead! Dead!" he repeated, with a bewildered air.

He stared at those fixed eyes, that grim mouth, that livid flesh, and that blood – all that blood which had flowed over the carpet and congealed there in thick, black spots. He arose and turned on the electric lights. Then he beheld all the marks of a desperate struggle. The bed was in a state of great disorder. On the floor, the candlestick, and the clock, with the hands pointing to twenty minutes after eleven; then, further away, an overturned chair; and, everywhere, there was blood, spots of blood and pools of blood.

"And the black pearl?" he murmured.

The box of letter paper was in its place. He opened it, eagerly. The jewel case was there, but it was empty.

"Fichtre!" he muttered. "You boasted of your good fortune much too soon, my friend Lupin. With the countess lying cold and dead, and the black pearl vanished, the situation is anything but pleasant. Get out of here as soon as you can, or you may get into serious trouble."

Yet, he did not move.

"Get out of here? Yes, of course. Any person would, except Arsène Lupin. He has something better to do. Now, to proceed in an orderly way. At all events, you have a clear conscience. Let us suppose that you are the commissary of police and that you are proceeding to make an inquiry concerning this affair. Yes, but in order to do that, I require a clearer brain. Mine is muddled like a ragout."

He tumbled into an armchair, with his clenched hands pressed against his burning forehead.

* * *

The murder of the avenue Hoche is one of those which have recently surprised and puzzled the Parisian public, and, certainly, I should never have mentioned the affair if the veil of mystery had not been removed by Arsène Lupin himself. No one knew the exact truth of the case.

Who did not know – from having met her in the Bois – the fair Léotine Zalti, the once famous cantatrice, wife and widow of the Count d'Andillot; the Zalti, whose luxury dazzled all Paris some twenty years ago; the Zalti who acquired a European reputation for the magnificence of her diamonds and pearls? It was said that she wore upon her shoulders the capital of several banking houses and the gold mines of numerous Australian companies. Skilful jewellers worked for Zalti as they had formerly wrought for kings and queens. And who does not remember the catastrophe in which all that wealth was swallowed up? Of all that marvellous collection, nothing remained except the famous black pearl. The black pearl! That is to say a fortune, if she had wished to part with it.

But she preferred to keep it, to live in a commonplace apartment with her companion, her cook, and a manservant, rather than sell that inestimable jewel. There was a reason for it; a reason she was not afraid to disclose: the black pearl was the gift of an emperor! Almost ruined, and reduced to the most mediocre existence, she remained faithful to the companion of her happy and brilliant youth. The black pearl never left her possession. She wore it during the day, and, at night, concealed it in a place known to her alone.

All these facts, being republished in the columns of the public press, served to stimulate curiosity; and, strange to say, but quite obvious to those who have the key to the mystery, the arrest of the presumed assassin only complicated the question and prolonged the excitement. Two days later, the newspapers published the following item:

Information has reached us of the arrest of Victor Danègre, the servant of the Countess d'Andillot. The evidence against him is clear and convincing. On the silken sleeve of his liveried waistcoat, which chief detective Dudouis found in his garret between the mattresses of his bed, several spots of blood were discovered. In addition, a cloth-covered button was missing from that garment, and this button was found beneath the bed of the victim.

It is supposed that, after dinner, in place of going to his own room, Danègre slipped into the wardrobe-closet, and, through the glass door, had seen the countess hide the precious black pearl. This is simply a theory, as yet unverified by any evidence. There is, also, another obscure point. At seven o'clock in the morning, Danègre went to the tobacco-shop on the Boulevard de Courcelles; the concierge and the shop-keeper both affirm this fact. On the other hand, the countess' companion and cook, who sleep at the end of the hall, both declare that, when they arose at eight o'clock, the door of the antechamber and the door of the kitchen were locked. These two persons have been in the service of the countess for twenty years, and are above suspicion. The question is: How did Danègre leave the apartment? Did he have another key? These are matters that the police will investigate.

As a matter of fact, the police investigation threw no light on the mystery. It was learned that Victor Danègre was a dangerous criminal, a drunkard and a debauchee. But, as they proceeded with the investigation, the mystery deepened and new complications arose. In the first place, a young woman, Mademoiselle De Sinclèves, the cousin and sole heiress of the countess, declared that the countess, a month before her death, had written a letter to her and in it described the manner in which the black pearl was concealed. The letter disappeared the day after she received it. Who had stolen it?

Again, the concierge related how she had opened the door for a person who had inquired for Doctor Harel. On being questioned, the doctor testified that no one had rung his bell. Then who was that person? An accomplice?

The theory of an accomplice was thereupon adopted by the press and public, and also by Ganimard, the famous detective.

"Lupin is at the bottom of this affair," he said to the judge.

"Bah!" exclaimed the judge, "you have Lupin on the brain. You see him everywhere."

"I see him everywhere, because he is everywhere."

"Say rather that you see him every time you encounter something you cannot explain. Besides, you overlook the fact that the crime was committed at twenty minutes past eleven in the evening, as is shown by the clock, while the nocturnal visit, mentioned by the concierge, occurred at three o'clock in the morning."

Officers of the law frequently form a hasty conviction as to the guilt of a suspected person, and then distort all subsequent discoveries to conform to their established theory. The deplorable antecedents of Victor Danègre, habitual criminal, drunkard and rake, influenced the judge, and despite the fact that nothing new was discovered in corroboration of the early clues, his official opinion remained firm and unshaken. He closed his investigation, and, a few weeks later, the trial commenced. It proved to be slow and tedious.

The judge was listless, and the public prosecutor presented the case in a careless manner. Under those circumstances, Danègre's counsel had an easy task. He pointed out the defects and inconsistencies of the case for the prosecution, and argued that the evidence was quite insufficient to convict the accused. Who had made the key, the indispensable key without which Danègre, on leaving the apartment, could not have locked the door behind him? Who had ever seen such a key, and what had become of it? Who had seen the assassin's knife, and where is it now?

"In any event," argued the prisoner's counsel, "the prosecution must prove, beyond any reasonable doubt, that the prisoner committed the murder. The prosecution must show that the mysterious individual who entered the house at three o'clock in the morning is not the guilty party. To be sure, the clock indicated eleven o'clock. But what of that? I contend, that proves nothing. The assassin could turn the hands of the clock to any hour he pleased, and thus deceive us in regard to the exact hour of the crime."

Victor Danègre was acquitted.

He left the prison on Friday about dusk in the evening, weak and depressed by his six months' imprisonment. The inquisition, the solitude, the trial, the deliberations of the jury, combined to fill him with a nervous fear. At night, he had been afflicted with terrible nightmares and haunted by weird visions of the scaffold. He was a mental and physical wreck.

Under the assumed name of Anatole Dufour, he rented a small room on the heights of Montmartre, and lived by doing odd jobs wherever he could find them. He led a pitiful existence. Three times, he obtained regular employment, only to be recognised and then discharged. Sometimes, he had an idea that men were following him – detectives, no doubt, who were seeking to trap and denounce him. He could almost feel the strong hand of the law clutching him by the collar.

One evening, as he was eating his dinner at a neighbouring restaurant, a man entered and took a seat at the same table. He was a person about forty years of age, and wore a frock coat of doubtful cleanliness. He ordered soup, vegetables, and a bottle of wine. After he had finished his soup, he turned his eyes on Danègre, and gazed at him intently. Danègre winced. He was certain that this was one of the men who had been following him for several weeks. What did he want? Danègre tried to rise, but failed. His limbs refused to support him. The man poured himself a glass of wine, and then filled Danègre's glass. The man raised his glass, and said:

"To your health, Victor Danègre."

Victor started in alarm, and stammered:

"I ... I! No, no ... I swear to you ..."

"You will swear what? That you are not yourself? The servant of the countess?"

"What servant? My name is Dufour. Ask the proprietor."

"Yes, Anatole Dufour to the proprietor of this restaurant, but Victor Danègre to the officers of the law."

"That's not true! Someone has lied to you."

The newcomer took a card from his pocket and handed it to Victor, who read on it: 'Grimaudan, ex-inspector of the detective force. Private business transacted.' Victor shuddered as he said:

"You are connected with the police?"

"No, not now, but I have a liking for the business and I continue to work at it in a manner more – profitable. From time to time I strike upon a golden opportunity – such as your case presents."

"My case?"

"Yes, yours. I assure you it is a most promising affair, provided you are inclined to be reasonable."

"But if I am not reasonable?"

"Oh! My good fellow, you are not in a position to refuse me anything I may ask."

"What is it ... you want?" stammered Victor, fearfully.

"Well, I will inform you in a few words. I am sent by Mademoiselle de Sinclèves, the heiress of the Countess d'Andillot."

"What for?"

"To recover the black pearl."

"Black pearl?"

"That you stole."

"But I haven't got it."

"You have it."

"If I had, then I would be the assassin."

"You are the assassin."

Danègre showed a forced smile.

"Fortunately for me, monsieur, the Assize Court was not of your opinion. The jury returned an unanimous verdict of acquittal. And when a man has a clear conscience and twelve good men in his favour–"

The ex-inspector seized him by the arm and said:

"No fine phrases, my boy. Now, listen to me and weigh my words carefully. You will find they are worthy of your consideration. Now, Danègre, three weeks before the murder, you abstracted the cook's key to the servants' door, and had a duplicate key made by a locksmith named Outard, 244 rue Oberkampf."

"It's a lie – it's a lie!" growled Victor. "No person has seen that key. There is no such key."

"Here it is."

After a silence, Grimaudan continued:

"You killed the countess with a knife purchased by you at the Bazar de la Republique on the same day as you ordered the duplicate key. It has a triangular blade with a groove running from end to end."

"That is all nonsense. You are simply guessing at something you don't know. No one ever saw the knife."

"Here it is."

Victor Danègre recoiled. The ex-inspector continued:

"There are some spots of rust upon it. Shall I tell you how they came there?"

"Well! You have a key and a knife. Who can prove that they belong to me?"

"The locksmith, and the clerk from whom you bought the knife. I have already refreshed their memories, and, when you confront them, they cannot fail to recognize you."

His speech was dry and hard, with a tone of firmness and precision. Danègre was trembling with fear, and yet he struggled desperately to maintain an air of indifference.

"Is that all the evidence you have?"

"Oh! No, not at all. I have plenty more. For instance, after the crime, you went out the same way you had entered. But, in the centre of the wardrobe-room, being seized by some sudden fear, you leaned against the wall for support."

"How do you know that? No one could know such a thing," argued the desperate man.

"The police know nothing about it, of course. They never think of lighting a candle and examining the walls. But if they had done so, they would have found on the white plaster a faint red spot, quite distinct, however, to trace in it the imprint of your thumb which you had pressed against the wall while it was wet with blood. Now, as you are well aware, under the Bertillon system, thumb marks are one of the principal means of identification."

Victor Danègre was livid; great drops of perspiration rolled down his face and fell upon the table. He gazed, with a wild look, at the strange man who had narrated the story of his crime as faithfully as if he had been an invisible witness to it. Overcome and powerless, Victor bowed his head. He felt that it was useless to struggle against this marvellous man. So he said:

"How much will you give me, if I give you the pearl?"

"Nothing."

"Oh! You are joking! Or do you mean that I should give you an article worth thousands and hundreds of thousands and get nothing in return?"

"You will get your life. Is that nothing?"

The unfortunate man shuddered. Then Grimaudan added, in a milder tone:

"Come, Danègre, that pearl has no value in your hands. It is quite impossible for you to sell it; so what is the use of your keeping it?"

"There are pawnbrokers ... and, some day, I will be able to get something for it."

"But that day may be too late."

"Why?"

"Because by that time you may be in the hands of the police, and, with the evidence that I can furnish – the knife, the key, the thumb mark – what will become of you?"

Victor rested his head on his hands and reflected. He felt that he was lost, irremediably lost, and, at the same time, a sense of weariness and depression overcame him. He murmured, faintly:

"When must I give it to you?"

"Tonight – within an hour."

"If I refuse?"

"If you refuse, I shall post this letter to the Procureur of the Republic; in which letter Mademoiselle de Sinclèves denounces you as the assassin."

Danègre poured out two glasses of wine which he drank in rapid succession, then, rising, said:

"Pay the bill, and let us go. I have had enough of the cursed affair."

Night had fallen. The two men walked down the rue Lepic and followed the exterior boulevards in the direction of the place de l'Etoile. They pursued their way in silence; Victor had a stooping carriage and a dejected face. When they reached the Parc Monceau, he said:

"We are near the house."

"Parbleu! You only left the house once, before your arrest, and that was to go to the tobacco shop."

"Here it is," said Danègre, in a dull voice.

They passed along the garden wall of the countess' house, and crossed a street on a corner of which stood the tobacco shop. A few steps further on, Danègre stopped; his limbs shook beneath him, and he sank to a bench.

"Well! What now?" demanded his companion.

"It is there."

"Where? Come, now, no nonsense!"

"There – in front of us."

"Where?"

"Between two paving stones."

"Which?"

"Look for it."

"Which stones?"

Victor made no reply.

"Ah; I see!" exclaimed Grimaudan, "you want me to pay for the information."

"No ... but ... I am afraid I will starve to death."

"So! That is why you hesitate. Well, I'll not be hard on you. How much do you want?"

"Enough to buy a steerage pass to America."

"All right."

"And a hundred francs to keep me until I get work there."

"You shall have two hundred. Now, speak."

"Count the paving stones to the right from the sewer-hole. The pearl is between the twelfth and thirteenth."

"In the gutter?"

"Yes, close to the sidewalk."

Grimaudan glanced around to see if anyone were looking. Some tram cars and pedestrians were passing. But, bah, they would not suspect anything. He opened his pocketknife and thrust it between the twelfth and thirteenth stones.

"And if it is not there?" he said to Victor.

"It must be there, unless someone saw me stoop down and hide it."

Could it be possible that the black pearl had been cast into the mud and filth of the gutter to be picked up by the firstcomer? The black pearl – a fortune!

"How far down?" he asked.

"About ten centimetres."

He dug up the wet earth. The point of his knife struck something. He enlarged the hole with his finger. Then he abstracted the black pearl from its filthy hiding place.

"Good! Here are your two hundred francs. I will send you the ticket for America."

On the following day, this article was published in the *Echo de France*, and was copied by the leading newspapers throughout the world:

Yesterday, the famous black pearl came into the possession of Arsène Lupin, who recovered it from the murderer of the Countess d'Andillot. In a short time, facsimiles of that precious jewel will be exhibited in London, St. Petersburg, Calcutta, Buenos Ayres and New York.

Arsène Lupin will be pleased to consider all propositions submitted to him through his agents.

* * *

"And that is how crime is always punished and virtue rewarded," said Arsène Lupin, after he had told me the foregoing history of the black pearl.

"And that is how you, under the assumed name of Grimaudan, ex-inspector of detectives, were chosen by fate to deprive the criminal of the benefit of his crime."

"Exactly. And I confess that the affair gives me infinite satisfaction and pride. The forty minutes that I passed in the apartment of the Countess d'Andillot, after learning of her death, were the most thrilling and absorbing moments of my life. In those forty minutes, involved as I was in a most dangerous plight, I calmly studied the scene of the murder and reached the conclusion that the crime must have been committed by one of the house servants. I also decided that, in order to get the pearl, that servant must be arrested, and so I left the wainscot button; it was necessary, also, for me to hold some convincing evidence of his guilt, so I carried away the knife which I found upon the floor, and the key which I found in the lock. I closed and locked the door, and erased the finger marks from the plaster in the wardrobe closet. In my opinion, that was one of those flashes—"

"Of genius," I said, interrupting.

"Of genius, if you wish. But, I flatter myself, it would not have occurred to the average mortal. To frame, instantly, the two elements of the problem – an arrest and an acquittal; to make use of the formidable machinery of the law to crush and humble my victim, and reduce him to a condition in which, when free, he would be certain to fall into the trap I was laying for him!"

"Poor devil–"

"Poor devil, do you say? Victor Danègre, the assassin! He might have descended to the lowest depths of vice and crime, if he had retained the black pearl. Now, he lives! Think of that: Victor Danègre is alive!"

"And you have the black pearl."

He took it out of one of the secret pockets of his wallet, examined it, gazed at it tenderly, and caressed it with loving fingers, and sighed, as he said:

"What cold Russian prince, what vain and foolish rajah may someday possess this priceless treasure! Or, perhaps, some American millionaire is destined to become the owner of this morsel of exquisite beauty that once adorned the fair bosom of Leontine Zalti, the Countess d'Andillot.

HERLOCK SHOLMES ARRIVES TOO LATE

"It is really remarkable, Velmont, what a close resemblance you bear to Arsène Lupin!"

"How do you know?"

"Oh! Like everyone else, from photographs, no two of which are alike, but each of them leaves the impression of a face ... something like yours."

Horace Velmont displayed some vexation.

"Quite so, my dear Devanne. And, believe me, you are not the first one who has noticed it."

"It is so striking," persisted Devanne, "that if you had not been recommended to me by my cousin d'Estevan, and if you were not the celebrated artist whose beautiful marine views I so admire, I have no doubt I should have warned the police of your presence in Dieppe."

This sally was greeted with an outburst of laughter. The large dining hall of the Château de Thibermesnil contained on this occasion, besides Velmont, the following guests: Father Gélis, the parish priest, and a dozen officers whose regiments were quartered in the vicinity and who had accepted the invitation of the banker Georges Devanne and his mother. One of the officers then remarked:

"I understand that an exact description of Arsène Lupin has been furnished to all the police along this coast since his daring exploit on the Paris-Havre express."

"I suppose so," said Devanne. "That was three months ago; and a week later, I made the acquaintance of our friend Velmont at the casino, and, since then, he has honoured me with several visits – an agreeable preamble to a more serious visit that he will pay me one of these days – or, rather, one of these nights."

This speech evoked another round of laughter, and the guests then passed into the ancient 'Hall of the Guards,' a vast room with a high ceiling, which occupied the entire lower part of the Tour Guillaume – William's Tower – and wherein Georges Devanne had collected the incomparable treasures which the lords of Thibermesnil had accumulated through many centuries. It contained ancient chests, credences, andirons and chandeliers. The stone walls were overhung with magnificent tapestries. The deep embrasures of the four windows were furnished with benches, and the Gothic windows were composed of small panes of coloured glass set in a leaden frame. Between the door and the window to the left stood an immense bookcase of Renaissance style, on the pediment of which, in letters of gold, was the word 'Thibermesnil, and, below it, the proud family device: 'Fais ce que veulx' (Do what thou wishest). When the guests had lighted their cigars, Devanne resumed the conversation.

"And remember, Velmont, you have no time to lose; in fact, tonight is the last chance you will have."

"How so?" asked the painter, who appeared to regard the affair as a joke. Devanne was about to reply, when his mother mentioned to him to keep silent, but the excitement of the occasion and a desire to interest his guests urged him to speak.

"Bah!" he murmured. "I can tell it now. It won't do any harm."

The guests drew closer, and he commenced to speak with the satisfied air of a man who has an important announcement to make.

"Tomorrow afternoon at four o'clock, Herlock Sholmes, the famous English detective, for whom such a thing as mystery does not exist; Herlock Sholmes, the most remarkable solver of enigmas the world has ever known, that marvellous man who would seem to be the creation of a romantic novelist – Herlock Sholmes will be my guest!"

Immediately, Devanne was the target of numerous eager questions. "Is Herlock Sholmes really coming?" "Is it so serious as that?" "Is Arsène Lupin really in this neighbourhood?"

"Arsène Lupin and his band are not far away. Besides the robbery of the Baron Cahorn, he is credited with the thefts at Montigny, Gruchet and Crasville. And now it is my turn."

"Has he sent you a warning, as he did to Baron Cahorn?"

"No," replied Devanne, "he can't work the same trick twice."

"What then?"

"I will show you."

He rose, and pointing to a small empty space between the two enormous folios on one of the shelves of the bookcase, he said:

"There used to be a book there – a book of the sixteenth century entitled *Chronique de Thibermesnil*, which contained the history of the castle since its construction by Duke Rollo on the site of a former feudal fortress. There were three engraved plates in the book; one of which was a general view of the whole estate; another, the plan of the buildings; and the third – I call your attention to it, particularly – the third was the sketch of a subterranean passage, an entrance to which is outside the first line of ramparts, while the other end of the passage is here, in this very room. Well, that book disappeared a month ago."

"The deuce!" said Velmont, "that looks bad. But it doesn't seem to be a sufficient reason for sending for Herlock Sholmes."

"Certainly, that was not sufficient in itself, but another incident happened that gives the disappearance of the book a special significance. There was another copy of this book in the National Library at Paris, and the two books differed in certain details relating to the subterranean passage; for instance, each of them contained drawings and annotations, not printed, but written in ink and more or less effaced. I knew those facts, and I knew that the exact location of the passage could be determined only by a comparison of the two books. Now, the day after my book disappeared, the book was called for in the National Library by a reader who carried it away, and no one knows how the theft was effected."

The guests uttered many exclamations of surprise.

"Certainly, the affair looks serious," said one.

"Well, the police investigated the matter, and, as usual, discovered no clue whatever."

"They never do, when Arsène Lupin is concerned in it."

"Exactly; and so I decided to ask the assistance of Herlock Sholmes, who replied that he was ready and anxious to enter the lists with Arsène Lupin."

"What glory for Arsène Lupin!" said Velmont. "But if our national thief, as they call him, has no evil designs on your castle, Herlock Sholmes will have his trip in vain."

"There are other things that will interest him, such as the discovery of the subterranean passage."

"But you told us that one end of the passage was outside the ramparts and the other was in this very room!"

"Yes, but in what part of the room? The line which represents the passage on the charts ends here, with a small circle marked with the letters 'T.G.,' which no doubt stand for 'Tour Guillaume.' But the tower is round, and who can tell the exact spot at which the passage touches the tower?"

Devanne lighted a second cigar and poured himself a glass of Benedictine. His guests pressed him with questions and he was pleased to observe the interest that his remarks had created. Then he continued:

"The secret is lost. No one knows it. The legend is to the effect that the former lords of the castle transmitted the secret from father to son on their deathbeds, until Geoffroy, the last of the race, was beheaded during the Revolution in his nineteenth year."

"That is over a century ago. Surely, someone has looked for it since that time?"

"Yes, but they failed to find it. After I purchased the castle, I made a diligent search for it, but without success. You must remember that this tower is surrounded by water and connected with the castle only by a bridge; consequently, the passage must be underneath the old moat. The plan that was in the book in the National Library showed a series of stairs with a total of forty-eight steps, which indicates a depth of more than ten meters. You see, the mystery lies within the walls of this room, and yet I do not wish to tear them down."

"Is there nothing to show where it is?"

"Nothing."

"Monsieur Devanne, we should turn our attention to the two quotations," suggested Father Gélis.

"Oh!" exclaimed Monsieur Devanne, laughing, "our worthy father is fond of reading memoirs and delving into the musty archives of the castle. Everything relating to Thibermesnil interests him greatly. But the quotations that he mentions only serve to complicate the mystery. He has read somewhere that two kings of France have known the key to the puzzle."

"Two kings of France! Who were they?"

"Henry the Fourth and Louis the Sixteenth. And the legend runs like this: On the eve of the battle of Arques, Henry the Fourth spent the night in this castle. At eleven o'clock in the evening, Louise de Tancarville, the prettiest woman in Normandy, was brought into the castle through the subterranean passage by Duke Edgard, who, at the same time, informed the king of the secret passage. Afterward, the king confided the secret to his minister Sully, who, in turn, relates the story in his book, *Royales Economies d'Etat*, without making any comment upon it, but linking with it this incomprehensible sentence: 'Turn one eye on the bee that shakes, the other eye will lead to God!'"

After a brief silence, Velmont laughed and said:

"Certainly, it doesn't throw a dazzling light upon the subject."

"No; but Father Gélis claims that Sully concealed the key to the mystery in this strange sentence in order to keep the secret from the secretaries to whom he dictated his memoirs."

"That is an ingenious theory," said Velmont.

"Yes, and it may be nothing more; I cannot see that it throws any light on the mysterious riddle."

"And was it also to receive the visit of a lady that Louis the Sixteenth caused the passage to be opened?"

"I don't know," said Monsieur Devanne. "All I can say is that the king stopped here one night in 1784, and that the famous Iron Casket found in the Louvre contained a paper bearing these words in the king's own writing: 'Thibermesnil 3-4-11.'"

Horace Velmont laughed heartily, and exclaimed:

"At last! And now that we have the magic key, where is the man who can fit it to the invisible lock?"

"Laugh as much as you please, monsieur," said Father Gélis, "but I am confident the solution is contained in those two sentences, and some day we will find a man able to interpret them."

"Herlock Sholmes is the man," said Monsieur Devanne,

"unless Arsène Lupin gets ahead of him. What is your opinion, Velmont?"

Velmont arose, placed his hand on Devanne's shoulder, and declared:

"I think that the information furnished by your book and the book of the National Library was deficient in a very important detail which you have now supplied. I thank you for it."

"What is it?"

"The missing key. Now that I have it, I can go to work at once," said Velmont.

"Of course; without losing a minute," said Devanne, smiling.

"Not even a second!" replied Velmont. "Tonight, before the arrival of Herlock Sholmes, I must plunder your castle."

"You have no time to lose. Oh! By the way, I can drive you over this evening."

"To Dieppe?"

"Yes. I am going to meet Monsieur and Madame d'Androl and a young lady of their acquaintance who are to arrive by the midnight train."

Then addressing the officers, Devanne added:

"Gentlemen, I shall expect to see all of you at breakfast tomorrow."

The invitation was accepted. The company dispersed, and a few moments later Devanne and Velmont were speeding toward Dieppe in an automobile. Devanne dropped the artist in front of the Casino, and proceeded to the railway station. At twelve o'clock his friends alighted from the train. A half hour later the automobile was at the entrance to the castle. At one o'clock, after a light supper, they retired. The lights were extinguished, and the castle was enveloped in the darkness and silence of the night.

* * *

The moon appeared through a rift in the clouds, and filled the drawing room with its bright white light. But only for a moment. Then the moon again retired behind its ethereal draperies, and darkness and silence reigned supreme. No sound could be heard, save the monotonous ticking of the clock. It struck two, and then continued its endless repetitions of the seconds. Then, three o'clock.

Suddenly, something clicked, like the opening and closing of a signal disc that warns the passing train. A thin stream of light flashed to every corner of the room, like an arrow that leaves behind it a trail of light. It shot forth from the central fluting of a column that supported the pediment of the bookcase. It rested for a moment on the panel opposite like a glittering circle of burnished silver, then flashed in all directions like a guilty eye that scrutinizes every shadow. It disappeared for a short time, but burst forth again as a whole section of the bookcase revolved on a pivot and disclosed a large opening like a vault.

A man entered, carrying an electric lantern. He was followed by a second man, who carried a coil of rope and various tools. The leader inspected the room, listened a moment, and said:

"Call the others."

Then eight men, stout fellows with resolute faces, entered the room, and immediately commenced to remove the furnishings. Arsène Lupin passed quickly from one piece of furniture to another, examined each, and, according to its size or artistic value, he directed his men to take it or leave it. If ordered to be taken, it was carried to the gaping mouth of the tunnel, and ruthlessly thrust into the bowels of the earth. Such was the fate of six armchairs, six small Louis XV chairs, a quantity of Aubusson tapestries, some candelabra, paintings by Fragonard and Nattier, a bust by Houdon, and some statuettes. Sometimes, Lupin would linger before a beautiful chest or a superb picture, and sigh:

"That is too heavy ... too large ... what a pity!"

In forty minutes, the room was dismantled; and it had been accomplished in such an orderly manner and with as little noise as if the various articles had been packed and wadded for the occasion.

Lupin said to the last man who departed by way of the tunnel:

"You need not come back. You understand, that as soon as the auto van is loaded, you are to proceed to the grange at Roquefort."

"But you, patron?"

"Leave me the motorcycle."

When the man had disappeared, Arsène Lupin pushed the section of the bookcase back into its place, carefully effaced the traces of the men's footsteps, raised a portière, and entered a gallery, which was the only means of communication between the tower and the castle. In the center of this gallery there was a glass cabinet which had attracted Lupin's attentions. It contained a valuable collection of watches, snuff-boxes, rings, chatelaines and miniatures of rare and beautiful workmanship. He forced the lock with a small jimmy, and experienced a great pleasure in handling those gold and silver ornaments, those exquisite and delicate works of art.

He carried a large linen bag, specially prepared for the removal of such knick-knacks. He filled it. Then he filled the pockets of his coat, waistcoat and trousers. And he was just placing over his left arm a number of pearl reticules when he heard a slight sound. He listened. No, he was not deceived. The noise continued. Then he remembered that, at one end of the gallery, there was a stairway leading to an unoccupied apartment, but which was probably occupied that night by the young lady whom Monsieur Devanne had brought from Dieppe with his other visitors.

Immediately he extinguished his lantern, and had scarcely gained the friendly shelter of a window-embrasure, when the door at the top of the stairway was opened and a feeble light illuminated the gallery. He could feel – for, concealed by a curtain, he could not see – that a woman was cautiously descending the upper steps of the stairs. He hoped she would come no closer. Yet, she continued to descend, and even advanced some distance into the room. Then she uttered a faint cry. No doubt she had discovered the broken and dismantled cabinet.

She advanced again. Now he could smell the perfume, and hear the throbbing of her heart as she drew closer to the window where he was concealed. She passed so close that her skirt brushed against the window-curtain, and Lupin felt that she suspected the presence of another, behind her, in the shadow, within reach of her hand. He thought: "She is afraid. She will go away." But she did not go. The candle, that she carried in her trembling hand, grew brighter. She turned, hesitated a moment, appeared to listen, then suddenly drew aside the curtain.

They stood face to face. Arsène was astounded. He murmured, involuntarily:

"You – you – mademoiselle."

It was Miss Nelly. Miss Nelly! His fellow passenger on the transatlantic steamer, who had been the subject of his dreams on that memorable voyage, who had been a witness to his arrest, and who, rather than betray him, had dropped into the water the Kodak in which he had concealed the banknotes and diamonds. Miss Nelly! That charming creature, the memory of whose face had sometimes cheered, sometimes saddened the long hours of imprisonment.

It was such an unexpected encounter that brought them face to face in that castle at that hour of the night, that they could not move, nor utter a word; they were amazed, hypnotized, each at the sudden apparition of the other. Trembling with emotion, Miss Nelly staggered to a seat. He remained standing in front of her.

Gradually, he realized the situation and conceived the impression he must have produced at that moment with his arms laden with knick-knacks, and his pockets and a linen sack overflowing with plunder. He was overcome with confusion, and he actually blushed to find himself in the position of a thief caught in the act. To her, henceforth, he was a thief, a man who puts his hand in another's pocket, who steals into houses and robs people while they sleep.

A watch fell upon the floor; then another. These were followed by other articles which slipped from his grasp one by one. Then, actuated by a sudden decision, he dropped the other articles into an armchair, emptied his pockets and unpacked his sack. He felt very uncomfortable in Nelly's presence, and stepped toward her with the intention of speaking to her, but she shuddered, rose quickly and fled toward the salon. The portière closed behind her. He followed her. She was standing trembling and amazed at the sight of the devastated room. He said to her, at once:

"Tomorrow, at three o'clock, everything will be returned. The furniture will be brought back."

She made no reply, so he repeated:

"I promise it. Tomorrow, at three o'clock. Nothing in the world could induce me to break that promise ... Tomorrow, at three o'clock."

Then followed a long silence that he dared not break, whilst the agitation of the young girl caused him a feeling of genuine regret. Quietly, without a word, he turned away, thinking: "I hope she will go away. I can't endure her presence." But the young girl suddenly spoke, and stammered:

"Listen ... footsteps ... I hear someone ..."

He looked at her with astonishment. She seemed to be overwhelmed by the thought of approaching peril.

"I don't hear anything," he said.

"But you must go – you must escape!"

"Why should I go?"

"Because – you must. Oh! do not remain here another minute. Go!"

She ran, quickly, to the door leading to the gallery and listened. No, there was no one there. Perhaps the noise was outside. She waited a moment, then returned reassured.

But Arsène Lupin had disappeared.

* * *

As soon as Monsieur Devanne was informed of the pillage of his castle, he said to himself: It was Velmont who did it, and Velmont is Arsène Lupin. That theory explained everything, and there was no other plausible explanation. And yet the idea seemed preposterous. It was ridiculous to suppose that Velmont was anyone else than Velmont, the famous artist, and club-fellow of his cousin d'Estevan. So, when the captain of the gendarmes arrived to investigate the affair, Devanne did not even think of mentioning his absurd theory.

Throughout the forenoon there was a lively commotion at the castle. The gendarmes, the local police, the chief of police from Dieppe, the villagers, all circulated to and fro in the halls, examining every nook and corner that was open to their inspection. The approach of the manoeuvring troops, the rattling fire of the musketry, added to the picturesque character of the scene.

The preliminary search furnished no clue. Neither the doors nor windows showed any signs of having been disturbed. Consequently, the removal of the goods must have been affected by means of the secret passage. Yet, there were no indications of footsteps on the floor, nor any unusual marks upon the walls.

Their investigations revealed, however, one curious fact that denoted the whimsical character of Arsène Lupin: the famous Chronique of the sixteenth century had been restored to its accustomed place in the library and, beside it, there was a similar book, which was none other than the volume stolen from the National Library.

At eleven o'clock the military officers arrived. Devanne welcomed them with his usual gaiety; for, no matter how much chagrin he might suffer from the loss of his artistic treasures, his great wealth enabled him to bear his loss philosophically. His guests, Monsieur and Madame d'Androl and Miss Nelly, were introduced; and it was then noticed that one of the expected guests had not arrived. It was Horace Velmont. Would he come? His absence had awakened the suspicions of Monsieur Devanne. But at twelve o'clock he arrived. Devanne exclaimed:

"Ah! Here you are!"

"Why, am I not punctual?" asked Velmont.

"Yes, and I am surprised that you are ... after such a busy night! I suppose you know the news?"

"What news?"

"You have robbed the castle."

"Nonsense!" exclaimed Velmont, smiling.

"Exactly as I predicted. But, first escort Miss Underdown to the dining-room. Mademoiselle, allow me—"

He stopped, as he remarked the extreme agitation of the young girl. Then, recalling the incident, he said:

"Ah! Of course, you met Arsène Lupin on the steamer, before his arrest, and you are astonished at the resemblance. Is that it?"

She did not reply. Velmont stood before her, smiling. He bowed. She took his proffered arm. He escorted her to her place, and took his seat opposite her. During the breakfast, the conversation related exclusively to Arsène Lupin, the stolen goods, the secret passage, and Herlock Sholmes. It was only at the close of the repast, when the conversation had drifted to other subjects, that Velmont took any part in it. Then he was, by turns, amusing and grave, talkative and pensive. And all his remarks seemed to be directed to the young girl. But she, quite absorbed, did not appear to hear them.

Coffee was served on the terrace overlooking the court of honour and the flower garden in front of the principal façade. The regimental band played on the lawn, and scores of soldiers and peasants wandered through the park.

Miss Nelly had not forgotten, for one moment, Lupin's solemn promise: "Tomorrow, at three o'clock, everything will be returned."

At three o'clock! And the hands of the great clock in the right wing of the castle now marked twenty minutes to three. In spite of herself, her eyes wandered to the clock every minute. She also watched Velmont, who was calmly swinging to and fro in a comfortable rocking chair.

Ten minutes to three ... Five minutes to three ...

Nelly was impatient and anxious. Was it possible that Arsène Lupin would carry out his promise at the appointed hour, when the castle, the courtyard, and the park were filled with people, and at the very moment when the officers of the law were pursuing their investigations? And yet ... Arsène Lupin had given her his solemn promise. "It will be exactly as he said," thought she, so deeply was she impressed with the authority, energy and assurance of that remarkable man. To her, it no longer assumed the form of a miracle, but, on the contrary, a natural incident that must occur in the ordinary course of events. She blushed, and turned her head.

Three o'clock! The great clock struck slowly: one ... two ... three ... Horace Velmont took out his watch, glanced at the clock, then returned the watch to his pocket. A few seconds passed in silence; and then the crowd in the courtyard parted to give passage to two wagons, that had just entered the park-gate, each drawn by two horses. They were army wagons, such as are used for the transportation of provisions, tents, and other necessary military stores. They stopped in front of the main entrance, and a commissary-sergeant leaped from one of the wagons and inquired for Monsieur Devanne. A moment later, that gentleman emerged from the house, descended the steps, and, under the canvas covers of the wagons, beheld his furniture, pictures and ornaments carefully packaged and arranged.

When questioned, the sergeant produced an order that he had received from the officer of the day. By that order, the second company of the fourth battalion were commanded to proceed to the crossroads of Halleux in the forest of Arques, gather up the furniture and other articles deposited there, and deliver same to Monsieur Georges Devanne, owner of the Thibermesnil castle, at three o'clock. Signed: Colonel Beauvel.

"At the crossroads," explained the sergeant, "we found everything ready, lying on the grass, guarded by some passers-by. It seemed very strange, but the order was imperative."

One of the officers examined the signature. He declared it a forgery; but a clever imitation. The wagons were unloaded, and the goods restored to their proper places in the castle.

During this commotion, Nelly had remained alone at the extreme end of the terrace, absorbed by confused and distracted thoughts. Suddenly, she observed Velmont approaching her. She would have avoided him, but the balustrade that surrounded the terrace cut off her retreat. She was cornered. She could not move. A gleam of sunshine, passing through the scant foliage of a bamboo, lighted up her beautiful golden hair. Someone spoke to her in a low voice:

"Have I not kept my promise?"

Arsène Lupin stood close to her. No one else was near. He repeated, in a calm, soft voice:

"Have I not kept my promise?"

He expected a word of thanks, or at least some slight movement that would betray her interest in the fulfilment of his promise. But she remained silent.

Her scornful attitude annoyed Arsène Lupin; and he realized the vast distance that separated him from Miss

Nelly, now that she had learned the truth. He would gladly have justified himself in her eyes, or at least pleaded extenuating circumstances, but he perceived the absurdity and futility of such an attempt. Finally, dominated by a surging flood of memories, he murmured:

"Ah! How long ago that was! You remember the long hours on the deck of the 'Provence'. Then, you carried a rose in your hand, a white rose like the one you carry today. I asked you for it. You pretended you did not hear me. After you had gone away, I found the rose – forgotten, no doubt – and I kept it."

She made no reply. She seemed to be far away. He continued:

"In memory of those happy hours, forget what you have learned since. Separate the past from the present. Do not regard me as the man you saw last night, but look at me, if only for a moment, as you did in those far-off days when I was Bernard d'Andrezy, for a short time. Will you, please?"

She raised her eyes and looked at him as he had requested. Then, without saying a word, she pointed to a ring he was wearing on his forefinger. Only the ring was visible; but the setting, which was turned toward the palm of his hand, consisted of a magnificent ruby. Arsène Lupin blushed. The ring belonged to Georges Devanne. He smiled bitterly, and said:

"You are right. Nothing can be changed. Arsène Lupin is now and always will be Arsène Lupin. To you, he cannot be even so much as a memory. Pardon me ... I should have known that any attention I may now offer you is simply an insult. Forgive me."

He stepped aside, hat in hand. Nelly passed before him. He was inclined to detain her and beseech her forgiveness. But his courage failed, and he contented himself by following her with his eyes, as he had done when she descended the gangway to the pier at New York. She mounted the steps leading to the door, and disappeared within the house. He saw her no more.

A cloud obscured the sun. Arsène Lupin stood watching the imprints of her tiny feet in the sand. Suddenly, he gave a start. Upon the box which contained the bamboo, beside which Nelly had been standing, he saw the rose, the white rose which he had desired but dared not ask for. Forgotten, no doubt – it, also! But how – designedly or through distraction? He seized it eagerly. Some of its petals fell to the ground. He picked them up, one by one, like precious relics.

"Come!" he said to himself, "I have nothing more to do here. I must think of my safety, before Herlock Sholmes arrives."

* * *

The park was deserted, but some gendarmes were stationed at the park gate. He entered a grove of pine trees, leaped over the wall, and, as a short cut to the railroad station, followed a path across the fields. After walking about ten minutes, he arrived at a spot where the road grew narrower and ran between two steep banks. In this ravine, he met a man travelling in the opposite direction. It was a man about fifty years of age, tall, smooth-shaven, and wearing clothes of a foreign cut.

He carried a heavy cane, and a small satchel was strapped across his shoulder. When they met, the stranger spoke, with a slight English accent:

"Excuse me, monsieur, is this the way to the castle?"

"Yes, monsieur, straight ahead, and turn to the left when you come to the wall. They are expecting you."

"Ah!"

"Yes, my friend Devanne told us last night that you were coming, and I am delighted to be the first to welcome you. Herlock Sholmes has no more ardent admirer than ... myself."

There was a touch of irony in his voice that he quickly regretted, for Herlock Sholmes scrutinized him from head to foot with such a keen, penetrating eye that Arsène Lupin experienced the sensation of being seized, imprisoned and registered by that look more thoroughly and precisely than he had ever been by a camera.

"My negative is taken now," he thought, "and it will be useless to use a disguise with that man. He would look right through it. But, I wonder, has he recognized me?"

They bowed to each other as if about to part. But, at that moment, they heard a sound of horses' feet, accompanied by a clinking of steel. It was the gendarmes. The two men were obliged to draw back against the embankment, amongst the brushes, to avoid the horses. The gendarmes passed by, but, as they followed each other at a considerable distance, they were several minutes in doing so. And Lupin was thinking:

"It all depends on that question: has he recognized me? If so, he will probably take advantage of the opportunity. It is a trying situation."

When the last horseman had passed, Herlock Sholmes stepped forth and brushed the dust from his clothes. Then, for a moment, he and Arsène Lupin gazed at each other; and, if a person could have seen them at that moment, it would have been an interesting sight, and memorable as the first meeting of two remarkable men, so strange, so powerfully equipped, both of superior quality, and destined by fate, through their peculiar attributes, to hurl themselves one at the other like two equal forces that nature opposes, one against the other, in the realms of space.

Then the Englishman said: "Thank you, monsieur."

"You are quite welcome, replied Arsène Lupin."

They parted. Lupin went toward the railway station, and Herlock Sholmes continued on his way to the castle.

The local officers had given up the investigation after several hours of fruitless efforts, and the people at the castle were awaiting the arrival of the English detective with a lively curiosity. At first sight, they were a little disappointed on account of his commonplace appearance, which differed so greatly from the pictures they had formed of him in their own minds. He did not in any way resemble the romantic hero, the mysterious and diabolical personage that the name of Herlock Sholmes had evoked in their imaginations. However, Monsieur Devanne exclaimed with much gusto:

"Ah! Monsieur, you are here! I am delighted to see you. It is a long-deferred pleasure. Really, I scarcely regret what has happened, since it affords me the opportunity to meet you. But, how did you come?"

"By the train."

"But I sent my automobile to meet you at the station."

"An official reception, eh? With music and fireworks! Oh! no, not for me. That is not the way I do business," grumbled the Englishman.

This speech disconcerted Devanne, who replied, with a forced smile:

"Fortunately, the business has been greatly simplified since I wrote to you."

"In what way?"

"The robbery took place last night."

"If you had not announced my intended visit, it is probable the robbery would not have been committed last night."

"When, then?"

"Tomorrow, or some other day."

"And in that case?"

"Lupin would have been trapped," said the detective.

"And my furniture?"

"Would not have been carried away."

"Ah! But my goods are here. They were brought back at three o'clock."

"By Lupin."

"By two army wagons."

Herlock Sholmes put on his cap and adjusted his satchel. Devanne exclaimed, anxiously:

"But, monsieur, what are you going to do?"

"I am going home."

"Why?"

"Your goods have been returned; Arsène Lupin is far away – there is nothing for me to do."

"Yes, there is. I need your assistance. What happened

yesterday, may happen again tomorrow, as we do not know how he entered, or how he escaped, or why, a few hours later, he returned the goods."

"Ah! You don't know–"

The idea of a problem to be solved quickened the interest of Herlock Sholmes.

"Very well, let us make a search – at once – and alone, if possible."

Devanne understood, and conducted the Englishman to the salon. In a dry, crisp voice, in sentences that seemed to have been prepared in advance, Sholmes asked a number of questions about the events of the preceding evening, and enquired also concerning the guests and the members of the household. Then he examined the two volumes of the *Chronique*, compared the plans of the subterranean passage, requested a repetition of the sentences discovered by Father Gélis, and then asked:

"Was yesterday the first time you have spoken those two sentences to any one?"

"Yes."

"You had never communicated them to Horace Velmont?"

"No."

"Well, order the automobile. I must leave in an hour."

"In an hour?"

"Yes; within that time, Arsène Lupin solved the problem that you placed before him."

"I ... placed before him–"

"Yes, Arsène Lupin or Horace Velmont – same thing."

"I thought so. Ah! The scoundrel!"

"Now, let us see," said Sholmes, "last night at ten o'clock, you furnished Lupin with the information that he lacked, and that he had been seeking for many weeks. During the night, he found time to solve the problem, collect his men, and rob the castle. I shall be quite as expeditious."

He walked from end to end of the room, in deep thought, then sat down, crossed his long legs and closed his eyes.

Devanne waited, quite embarrassed. Thought he: "Is the man asleep? Or is he only meditating?" However, he left the room to give some orders, and when he returned he found the detective on his knees scrutinizing the carpet at the foot of the stairs in the gallery.

"What is it?" he enquired.

"Look ... there ... spots from a candle."

"You are right – and quite fresh."

"And you will also find them at the top of the stairs, and around the cabinet that Arsène Lupin broke into, and from which he took the bibelots that he afterward placed in this armchair."

"What do you conclude from that?"

"Nothing. These facts would doubtless explain the cause for the restitution, but that is a side issue that I cannot wait to investigate. The main question is the secret passage. First, tell me, is there a chapel some two or three hundred metres from the castle?"

"Yes, a ruined chapel, containing the tomb of Duke Rollo."

"Tell your chauffeur to wait for us near that chapel."

"My chauffeur hasn't returned. If he had, they would have informed me. Do you think the secret passage runs to the chapel? What reason have–"

"I would ask you, monsieur," interrupted the detective, "to furnish me with a ladder and a lantern."

"What! Do you require a ladder and a lantern?"

"Certainly, or I shouldn't have asked for them."

Devanne, somewhat disconcerted by this crude logic, rang the bell. The two articles were given with the sternness and precision of military commands.

"Place the ladder against the bookcase, to the left of the word Thibermesnil."

Devanne placed the ladder as directed, and the Englishman continued:

"More to the left ... to the right ... There! Now, climb up ... All the letters are in relief, aren't they?"

"Yes."

"First, turn the letter 'I' one way or the other."

"Which one? There are two of them."

"The first one."

Devanne took hold of the letter, and exclaimed:

"Ah! Yes, it turns toward the right. Who told you that?"

Herlock Sholmes did not reply to the question,

but continued his directions:

"Now, take the letter 'B'. Move it back and forth as you would a bolt."

Devanne did so, and, to his great surprise, it produced a clicking sound.

"Quite right," said Sholmes. "Now, we will go to the other end of the word Thibermesnil, try the letter 'I', and see if it will open like a wicket."

With a certain degree of solemnity, Devanne seized the letter. It opened, but Devanne fell from the ladder, for the entire section of the bookcase, lying between the first and last letters of the words, turned on a pivot and disclosed the subterranean passage.

Herlock Sholmes said, coolly:

"You are not hurt?"

"No, no," said Devanne, as he rose to his feet, "not hurt, only bewildered. I can't understand now ... those letters turn ... the secret passage opens ..."

"Certainly. Doesn't that agree exactly with the formula given by Sully? Turn one eye on the bee that shakes, the other eye will lead to God."

"But Louis the sixteenth?" asked Devanne.

"Louis the sixteenth was a clever locksmith. I have read a book he wrote about combination locks. It was a good idea on the part of the owner of Thibermesnil to show His Majesty a clever bit of mechanism. As an aid to his memory, the king wrote: 3-4-11, that is to say, the third, fourth and eleventh letters of the word."

"Exactly. I understand that. It explains how Lupin got out of the room, but it does not explain how he entered. And it is certain he came from the outside."

Herlock Sholmes lighted his lantern, and stepped into the passage.

"Look! All the mechanism is exposed here, like the works of a clock, and the reverse side of the letters can be reached. Lupin worked the combination from this side – that is all."

"What proof is there of that?"

"Proof? Why, look at that puddle of oil. Lupin foresaw that the wheels would require oiling."

"Did he know about the other entrance?"

"As well as I know it," said Sholmes. "Follow me."

"Into that dark passage?"

"Are you afraid?"

"No, but are you sure you can find the way out?"

"With my eyes closed."

At first, they descended twelve steps, then twelve more, and, farther on, two other flights of twelve steps each. Then they walked through a long passageway, the brick walls of which showed the marks of successive restorations, and, in spots, were dripping with water. The earth, also, was very damp.

"We are passing under the pond," said Devanne, somewhat nervously.

At last, they came to a stairway of twelve steps, followed by three others of twelve steps each, which they mounted with difficulty, and then found themselves in a small cavity cut in the rock. They could go no further.

"The deuce!" muttered Sholmes, "nothing but bare walls. This is provoking."

"Let us go back," said Devanne. "I have seen enough to satisfy me."

But the Englishman raised his eye and uttered a sigh of relief. There, he saw the same mechanism and the same word as before. He had merely to work the three letters. He did so, and a block of granite swung out of place. On the other side, this granite block formed the tombstone of Duke Rollo, and the word 'Thibermesnil' was engraved on it in relief. Now, they were in the little ruined chapel, and the detective said:

"The other eye leads to God; that means, to the chapel."

"It is marvellous!" exclaimed Devanne, amazed at the clairvoyance and vivacity of the Englishman. "Can it be possible that those few words were sufficient for you?"

"Bah!" declared Sholmes, "they weren't even necessary. In the chart in the book of the National Library, the drawing terminates at the left, as you know, in a circle, and at the right, as you do not know, in a cross. Now, that cross must refer to the chapel in which we now stand."

Poor Devanne could not believe his ears. It was all so new, so novel to him. He exclaimed:

"It is incredible, miraculous, and yet of a childish simplicity! How is it that no one has ever solved the mystery?"

"Because no one has ever united the essential elements, that is to say, the two books and the two sentences. No one, but Arsène Lupin and myself."

"But, Father Gélis and I knew all about those things, and, likewise–"

Sholmes smiled, and said:

"Monsieur Devanne, everybody cannot solve riddles."

"I have been trying for ten years to accomplish what you did in ten minutes."

"Bah! I am used to it."

They emerged from the chapel, and found an automobile.

"Ah! There's an auto waiting for us."

"Yes, it is mine," said Devanne.

"Yours? You said your chauffeur hadn't returned."

They approached the machine, and Monsieur Devanne questioned the chauffeur:

"Edouard, who gave you orders to come here?"

"Why, it was Monsieur Velmont."

"Monsieur Velmont? Did you meet him?"

"Near the railway station, and he told me to come to the chapel."

"To come to the chapel! What for?"

"To wait for you, monsieur, and your friend."

Devanne and Sholmes exchanged looks, and Monsieur Devanne said:

"He knew the mystery would be a simple one for you. It is a delicate compliment."

A smile of satisfaction lighted up the detective's serious features for a moment. The compliment pleased him. He shook his head, as he said:

"A clever man! I knew that when I saw him."

"Have you seen him?"

"I met him a short time ago – on my way from the station."

"And you knew it was Horace Velmont – I mean, Arsène Lupin?"

"That is right. I wonder how it came–"

"No, but I supposed it was – from a certain ironical speech he made."

"And you allowed him to escape?"

"Of course I did. And yet I had everything on my side, such as five gendarmes who passed us."

"Sacrableu!" cried Devanne. "You should have taken advantage of the opportunity."

"Really, monsieur," said the Englishman, haughtily, "when I encounter an adversary like Arsène Lupin, I do not take advantage of chance opportunities, I create them."

But time pressed, and since Lupin had been so kind as to send the automobile, they resolved to profit by it. They seated themselves in the comfortable limousine;

Edouard took his place at the wheel, and away they went toward the railway station. Suddenly, Devanne's eyes fell upon a small package in one of the pockets of the carriage.

"Ah! What is that? A package! Whose is it? Why, it is for you."

"For me?"

"Yes, it is addressed: Herlock Sholmes, from Arsène Lupin."

The Englishman took the package, opened it, and found that it contained a watch.

"Ah!" he exclaimed, with an angry gesture.

"A watch," said Devanne. "How did it come there?"

The detective did not reply.

"Oh! It is your watch! Arsène Lupin returns your watch! But, in order to return it, he must have taken it. Ah! I see! He took your watch! That is a good one! Herlock Sholmes' watch stolen by Arsène Lupin! Mon Dieu! that is funny! Really ... you must excuse me ... I can't help it."

He roared with laughter, unable to control himself. After which, he said, in a tone of earnest conviction:

"A clever man, indeed!"

The Englishman never moved a muscle. On the way to Dieppe, he never spoke a word, but fixed his gaze on the flying landscape. His silence was terrible, unfathomable, more violent than the wildest rage. At the railway station, he spoke calmly, but in a voice that impressed one with the vast energy and will power of that famous man. He said:

"Yes, he is a clever man, but someday I shall have the pleasure of placing on his shoulder the hand I now offer to you, Monsieur Devanne. And I believe that Arsène Lupin and Herlock Sholmes will meet again some day. Yes, the world is too small – we will meet – we must meet – and then–"